D1709369

SASQUATCH

AND THE GREEN SASH

A ROMANCE

KEITH HENDERSON

SASQUATCH
AND THE GREEN SASH

A ROMANCE

LIVRES
DC
BOOKS

Illustrations by Steve Adams.
Book designed and typeset by Primeau Barey, Montreal.

Copyright © Keith Henderson, 2018.
Legal Deposit, Bibliothèque et Archives nationales du Québec
and Library and Archives Canada, 3rd trimester, 2018.

Library and Archives Canada Cataloguing in Publication
Henderson, Keith, 1945- , author
Sasquatch and the green sash: a romance / Keith Henderson.
Introductory essay by K. S. Whetter. Illustrations by Steve Adams.
Adaptation of: Sir Gawain and the Green Knight.
Includes bibliographical references.
ISBN 978-1-927599-40-2 (hardcover)
I. Whetter, K. S. (Kevin Sean), 1969- , writer of introduction
II. Adams, Steve, 1967-, illustrator III. Title.
IV. Title: Sir Gawain and the Green Knight.
PS8565.E555S27 2018   C813'.54   C2018-904981-2

For our publishing activities, DC Books gratefully acknowledges the financial
support of SODEC and of the Government of Canada through Canadian Heritage
and the Canada Book Fund. *Nous reconnaissons l'aide financière du gouvernement
du Canada.*

Printed and bound in Canada.
Distributed by Fitzhenry and Whiteside.

Société
de développement
des entreprises
culturelles
Québec

Canada

DC Books
5 Fenwick Ave., Montreal West
Quebec H4X 1P3
www.dcbooks.ca

INTRODUCTORY ESSAY

K. S. Whetter
Acadia University

Sasquatch and the Green Sash (as anybody reading this essay already knows) is subtitled "a romance," and Keith Henderson evokes "the most reputable books of romance" at his story's conclusion. Accordingly, my prefatory remarks are concerned partly with a discussion of the genre announced by that subtitle and invocation, as well as with some explanation of the most reputable mediaeval subtext that underlies the story. I shall close by speaking to some of the ways in which Henderson incorporates his source into a very Canadian context and mythology.

Romance is the most capacious and arguably most misunderstood of literary genres, partly because its parameters change somewhat depending on whether one is discussing the Greek romance-novels of the Classical world (Xenophon of Ephesus's *Habrocomes and Antheia* or Longus's *Daphnis and Chloe*, both in the third or second century), mediaeval romances of Tristan and Iseult (popularized by various poets from the twelfth century on before being turned into prose in the thirteenth and fifteenth centuries) or Gawain and Dame Ragnell (circa 1450), or the early modern romances that eventually morphed into the early novel. It is therefore perhaps best to begin with what romance is not: despite the eventual evolution from late-mediaeval romance into the early novel, and despite several thematic connections between the two genres, romance is not a novel and approaching it with novelistic expectations will only lead to disappointment. Despite the similarities of name, mediaeval romance as a genre is also distinct from Romantic literature, that is to say, the poetry, prose, or essays that we associate with the period in English and European literature between roughly 1770 and 1848 and with authors such as William Wordsworth (1770-1850), William Blake (1757-1827), or Mary Wollstonecraft (1759-97). Finally, mediaeval romance is not the same as the modern genre often classified as Harlequin or Mills and Boon romance novels, one type of which Gordon Lightfoot refers to as "a paperback novel [of] / The kind the drugstores sell." The plot features of love and adventure are common to romances of all eras, but these generic elements unfold in a different fashion in mediaeval romance than in other kinds.

If the romance genre is not these things, what is it then? That is a question which has occupied–and divided–literary critics for over a hundred years. The great Canadian scholar Northrop Frye once described romance as "the secular scripture," a statement which gives us some sense of romance's importance and audience. (For a list of sources and scholarly recommendations, see the items listed in the Further Reading bibliography at the end of this Introduction). Romance in general is *secular* because throughout its literary history, and especially in the Middle Ages, it tends to be distinct from religious or morally didactic literature; romance may try to teach us something, but it is primarily a genre of entertainment akin to modern action movies or mid-twentieth-century Westerns rather than independent films or documentaries. Indeed, in the Middle Ages, romance was *the* pree-minent literary form of entertainment, one whose secularity is evident in the genre's association with the gentry and aristocracy. Although mediaeval romance was most likely popular with various social classes, it is, notoriously, a genre dominated by deeds of knights and ladies or kings and queens, an idealized–and at times searching–self-portrait of the knightly class. Romance is a *scripture* because of its popularity and the wide-spread appeal and understanding of its dominant themes. To turn again to the mediaeval romance, although some romances were written in Latin, the majority were popular in part because they were written in what are called the vernacular languages (French, English, Spanish, Dutch, German, Old Norse, Old Swedish, Icelandic, etc.); indeed, etymologically, the very word *roman* refers to a story written in the (French) vernacular. Mediaeval romance also exists in a variety of forms, from verse to prose, short to long narratives, and in both popular and high-brow manifestations. Arthurian romance alone – to say nothing of other types – existed (and survives) in all countries and languages across mediaeval Europe, including French, Dutch, Portuguese, German, English, Welsh, Norse, and Italian examples.

Frye's conception of romance as a secular scripture was meant to apply to the genre in the widest sense and was a development of Frye's deservedly influential study of literature on the basis of recurring genres, tropes, and archetypes in his *Anatomy of Criticism*. Responding to the Greek philosopher-critic Aristotle's focus on plot as the driving force of genre, Frye instead classifies "literary fictions" on the basis of "the hero's power of action, which may be greater than ours, less, or roughly the same." For all the strengths of Frye's theory of archetypes and genres, most of his examples of romance are taken from before or after the Middle Ages: Classical literature, Elizabethan, or Nineteenth-century prose authors. By this account even Homer's *Odyssey* (circa 700 BCE), which is an epic poem with a qualified happy ending, is sometimes misleadingly considered a romance because of its focus on adventure, monsters, and family reunions. Mediaeval romance, however, is not quite the same as these other examples.

By an archetypal account, romance can be considered a fictional narrative operating in a world almost but not quite the same as our own, focussing on characters whose attributes and actions, prowess, endurance, and beauty, may not be entirely realistic. This lack of

realism long haunted romance, garnering both wide-spread popular appeal and wide-spread scholarly derision. Mediaeval romances
greatly influenced Victorian authors and artists, notably Alfred Lord
Tennyson (1809-92) and William Morris (1834-96), and attracted
many Victorian intellectuals as well as general readers. Although many
early twentieth-century critics tended to dismiss mediaeval romance as
too formulaic and repetitive, as well as too unrealistic, to be regarded as
anything other than low-brow, more sympathetic scholarship eventually won out and mediaeval romance today is widely studied in its own
right as not merely popular but successful and interesting literature.
It is also increasingly recognized by scholars as a window onto chivalric culture. But because mediaeval romance exists in a wide range of
languages, in forms both long and short and in verse or prose, covering
a disparate range of subjects and characters, it has proven remarkably
controversial to define. Indeed, some experts have suggested that we
cannot define the genre and should not try. It is, however, unfair to
students or readers to classify a narrative as "romance" and then claim
that romance must simply be recognized rather than defined. Thus,
although not all scholars agree with me, and although there are always
exceptions to any generic rule, I contend that there is sufficient literary
evidence and sufficient literary-critical agreement to say that mediaeval
romance can be recognized and defined on the basis of several distinct
and recurring literary features. Other elements of plot or narrative
feature may also appear frequently in romance, but these *essential* and
recurring features define the genre. One such essential romance feature
is the specific *characters*, who tend to be upper-class, generally knights
and ladies or even kings and queens. (Henderson updates the knightly
protagonist to a young Mountie in the Northwest Territories.) The
plot of romance tends to be driven by *adventure*, generally chivalric
or knightly adventure in the forms of tournaments, battles, or fights

with monstrous foes, though some romances have a woman as the main character and so pursue slightly different adventures. (The adventure in *Sasquatch and the Green Sash*, as often in Arthurian romance, is started by a challenger entering Arthur's court, and Henderson's challenger, who is also part giant, bears an impressive sword, thereby instigating a mediaeval rather than modern adventure.) Although some romance adventures happen randomly, the most significant have specific motivations. Thus, for instance, *women* play a leading role in instigating or defining the male action in romance, and *love* is a central factor motivating the characters. Generally, this love is heterosexual but sometimes it takes the form of love of fellowship or platonic bonds between people of the same sex. (Henderson's Gavin and Arthur, like their mediaeval counterparts, are related by blood and affection, but Gavin also meets a beautiful stranger; and has a significant woman in his past.) Finally, most romances *end happily*. Having said this, and as a prime example of literary exceptions to the generic rule, there is a prominent sub-set or sub-genre of mediaeval romances, including several Arthurian romances, that complicate the happy ending: I myself consider such tales as deliberate generic mixtures or *tragic romances*, but other scholars (notably Helen Cooper), argue for the commonality of unhappy happy endings.

Romance, then, was a popular genre across mediaeval Europe, with romance heroes including characters as diverse as Guy of Warwick (a knight who falls in love with a woman above his station and who sets off–successfully–to become famous enough to earn her hand in marriage), Bevis of Hampton (the son of an earl and an evil princess whose story involves pirates, Saracens, love, family reunions, and a special horse), Floris and Blancheflour (childhood sweethearts separated by his parents and reunited by Floris's quest for his beloved), William of Palerne (a king's son who is taken from home by a protective werewolf and who eventually becomes involved in a love match with Melior, the Emperor's daughter), or the beautiful and pure Emare (who is subjected to both unwanted and reciprocated loves and various hardships). A popular sub-set of romances, one again evident across mediaeval Europe, were those devoted to the legend of King Arthur, including the initially separate Tristan and Iseult story that eventually got incorporated into the Arthurian orbit. In all cases, romance as a genre tends to focus on the adventures and crises and maturation of one individual protagonist. Other characters are also present, and many interact regularly with the hero – but romance spotlights one principal protagonist. Hence, in *Sasquatch and the Green Sash*, although there are a number of characters encountered, many of whom assist the hero and many of whom are important, the leading character is Gavin McHenry.

Like romance, the mediaeval Arthurian legend was a pan-European phenomenon and is consequently too diverse and too widespread to lend itself to easy summary or even highlights. I will thus confine my remaining comments to material useful for contextualizing *Sasquatch and the Green Sash*. As Keith Henderson makes perfectly clear, the modern romance *Sasquatch and the Green Sash* is an adaptation of the mediaeval romance *Sir Gawain and the Green Knight*. *Sir Gawain and the Green Knight* is almost universally beloved by literary specialists and teachers, is a staple of undergraduate English literature university courses, and is arguably the finest Arthurian romance produced in any language in the Middle Ages. Unsurprisingly, then, the poem has spawned several modern cinematic and literary adaptations, including in comics or graphic novels; most of the cinematic adaptations, however, are at best mediocre, even when the Green Knight is played by Sean Connery (in the 1985 Cannon Group production *Sword of the Valiant*).

Despite its modern fame, scholars have been unable to determine who composed *Sir Gawain and the Green Knight*. In marked contrast to modern authors, mediaeval authors frequently failed to put their name to their work, and the identities of many mediaeval authors are unknown. Likewise, many mediaeval poems are untitled in the manuscripts that preserve them, with many titles for standard mediaeval works being the creation of modern (mostly nineteenth-century) editors. This is certainly the case with all fours poems in the mediaeval manuscript now known as London, British Library, MS Cotton Nero A.x, art. 3, the small and unelaborate manuscript in which the only mediaeval copy of *Sir Gawain and the Green Knight* survives. Stylistic and linguistic commonalities shared by all four poems – *Pearl*, *Cleanness* (sometimes called *Purity*), *Patience*, and Sir *Gawain and the Green Knight* – make literary critics reasonably certain that they are the product of the same author, but no one has succeeded in identifying who that author might have been. Since the two finest poems in the manuscript are *Sir Gawain and the Green Knight* and *Pearl*, our unknown author is accordingly referred to either as "the *Gawain*-poet" or "the *Pearl*-poet."

We have a somewhat better sense of the provenance of the mediaeval poem that inspires Henderson's work. *Sir Gawain and the Green Knight* is written in Middle English (roughly, the language between *Beowulf* and Shakespeare, more specifically from approximately 1100-1500) and is generally hailed as one of the jewels in the crown of the so-called fourteenth-century Alliterative Revival, a period in English verse where, for whatever reason, there suddenly appear once again in written form poems whose narrative and structure is carried not by rhyme or iambic rhythm but by alliteration: the repetition of sounds across the same line (and sometimes, with skilled poets, across several lines). Other features, including descriptions of architecture and clothing in the poem, including armour, allow us to date *Sir Gawain and the Green*

Knight to roughly the last quarter of the fourteenth century; beyond that, it is impossible to be certain. The dialect of the poem is North-West Midlands, more specifically south Cheshire-north Staffordshire, a dialect quite different from Geoffrey Chaucer's (circa 1343-1400) contemporary London English. As a result, and also because of the poet's awareness of details of architecture and hunting, as well as the knowledge of other courtly pastimes and merchandise evident in the text, some specialists place the poem's composition and initial audience in a provincial but noble household, probably in Cheshire itself, *perhaps* a court of one of Richard II's (reigned 1377-99) greater magnates. Not everyone agrees with this Ricardian suggestion, though, and the whole issue of the poem's precise milieu remains contentious.

Given both the power of the poem and the uncertainties of its provenance, the contexts and meaning of *Sir Gawain and the Green Knight* can be discussed at length. It is best, therefore, to turn to some specifics that may be of use to readers interested in *Sasquatch and the Green Sash*. First, the poem is structured around two notable motifs, the Beheading Game and the Exchange of Winnings motif, both of which re-appear in *Sasquatch and the Green Sash*, though Henderson cleverly adds a guessing game into the mix. Second, *Sir Gawain and the Green Knight* is a markedly *intertextual* story: that is, the poet was well-versed in French and English Arthurian stories, and part of the effect and indeed meaning of the narrative relies on the audience taking certain things for granted and the poet expecting the audience to have certain expectations. This intertextuality is likewise adopted and adapted by Henderson—to good effect.

Related to the poem's intertextuality, its talking to or asking its audience to keep in mind other Arthurian narratives whilst judging the one at hand, is the fact that *Sir Gawain and the Green Knight* comes relatively late in a long line of Arthurian romances devoted to Gawain,

SASQUATCH AND THE GREEN SASH

the nephew—on the sister's side—of King Arthur. The position of sister's son was important in some mediaeval cultures, and most mediaeval traditions agree that Gawain is one of the greatest knights in Arthur's court, though in the French tradition he is eventually supplanted by Lancelot and, in certain French stories, he devolves from hero to murderous thug. In the English Arthurian tradition, however, partly excepting Sir Thomas Malory's *Le Morte Darthur* (sic; completed 1469-70), Gawain is Arthur's greatest knight, a reputation and stature he holds at the start of *Sir Gawain and the Green Knight*. Equally, in both French and English romance, Gawain is not only a great fighter but a famous ladies' man. Romance knights are typically inspired by the love of one particular woman, most famously Lancelot's love of Guinevere (and vice versa). Gawain, however, is linked to no particular lady for any length of time: even in *The Weddynge of Syr Gawen and Dame Ragnelle*, although he is briefly married to Ragnelle, the poem ends with her death, thereby allowing Gawen to return to his famous life of multiple adventures and equally multiple amorous encounters. The *Gawain*-poet plays with this tradition of Gawain as an eager and much sought-after lover; so too does Henderson.

The last thing a modern audience needs to know of the mediaeval poem that inspires *Sasquatch and the Green Sash* is that the poet seems deliberately to be playing tricks on his audience. As noted, the poem is widely accepted as one of the greatest mediaeval romances; part of its greatness lies in its complexity and subtlety, including the poet's manipulation of the genre and of audience expectations. All of these elements come to a head in what is *the* great unresolved question of the poem: does Gawayn (as one of the Middle English spellings of the hero's name goes) succeed or fail in his test, and if he fails, how bad or qualified might that failure be? A knight whose five-fold virtues are defined and symbolized by the "pentangle" or "endless knot" (literally "pentangel" and "endeles knot": lines 619-39) is partly brought down by the green girdle or sash which likewise comes to symbolize his failures–or his qualified success.

One of the things that J. R. R. Tolkien most admired about *Sir Gawain and the Green Knight* was what Tolkien considered its *rootedness*, its sense of history and belonging to the past–and, of course, with the ways in which the modern student is drawn into that past when reading the poem. The detailed description the poet gives of Gawain's shield and the pentangle, including the pentangle's suitability as a symbol of Gawain's perfection and heroism, is one example of this kind of rootedness. At the same time, the pentangle also bespeaks the poet's originality, since literary specialists know of no other Arthurian story in which Gawain bears such a device on his shield. *Sir Gawain and the Green Knight* is also the first recorded appearance in English of the word *pentangle*, so again the poem (and the word) is and is not traditional here. The point of this brief discussion of *rootedness* in the poem is to suggest that Henderson, too, gives his story a sense of depth and belonging. For one thing, Henderson's nods to the Arthurian Legend in general and *Sir Gawain and the Green Knight* in particular are many; some of these allusions are themselves quite subtle. The story begins, for instance, in the "vast log cabin castle" of "Arthur LeMagne" of "Chamelot," and the alliteration of the original poem is carried through in phrases such as that used to introduce Henderson's Guinevere-figure: "Ghylaine, glinting and grey of eye." And several names of the chiefs in the Dene council (Eric, Dodinal, Belvidere, Bors, and Lionel) are inspired by Arthurian originals but transplanted to an indigenous culture and context. Indeed, the inclusion of the Dene Nation is one prominent example of the Canadian contextualization of the mediaeval story, as is the multicultural nature of Arthur LeMagne's court in his cabin under the aurora borealis where the guests feast on "blue goose and moose liver, bear steaks dripping with fat, and the finest cuts of bison and Dall sheep, a veritable *Ordre de Bon Temps*." Multiculturalism and rooted-ness are again apparent in the subtle Muslim connection evident at the climax of the story, where Gavin learns that his challenger's many names include "Wodwo" in Britain but "Al Khidr" in the East. "Wodwos" or "woodwose" is an Old English word meaning "wild man of the woods," and is a word found at line 721 of *Sir Gawain and the Green Knight*; it is also a word used, deliberately albeit with some modification, in Tolkien's Middle-earth writings. Al-Khidr, on the other hand, is figure of Islamic legend who is green and immortal and a teacher or guide; a select few scholars posit him as a possible source – or analogue – for the Green Knight. Regardless of the validity of this claim, the appearance of al-Khidr in *Sasquatch* certainly adds to the story's depth, simultaneously alerting readers to the fact that Henderson has done his homework: like the *Gawain*-poet, he is knowledgeable about the stories behind the story. Gavin, on the other hand, is a member of that most iconically Canadian establishment, the Royal Canadian Mounted Police, and his superior officer attends Arthur's feast in full red regalia. Skidoos are also present, but are not appropriate for questing, so Henderson manages to work in sled dogs – a suitably Northern stand-in for the traditional horse of the mediaeval questing knight. More subtle but no less important in the Canadian mythos is Henderson's use of language. Since I mentioned the etymology of *romans* earlier, it is worth noting now that, according to *The Canadian Encyclopedia*, the "word *Sasquatch* is believed to be an Anglicization of the Salish word *Sasq'ets*." In these and other ways, Henderson roots *Sasquatch and the Green sash* in both the mediaeval Arthurian past but also in the Canadian North.

A recurring component of the modern story's rootedness is the manner in which Henderson frequently carries over lines or scenes or even textual cruxes from the mediaeval poem. I cannot mention the most important of these borrowings without spoiling the plot, but a safe example is from the beginning of the story. Although the poem comes later in the Arthurian tradition as a whole, it is set early, when Arthur and his court are young: hence the Sasquatch's taunt near the beginning that he is not looking for a fight "since I see mostly beardless boys about anyway," an insult carried over straight from the poem and the Middle English phrase "berdlez chylder" (line 280). At the same time, Henderson must provide a modern audience with more psychological characterization, more insight into the protagonist's inner thoughts and demons, than is the norm in mediaeval romances. I do not myself subscribe to the view of some specialists that mediaeval romancers were uninterested in characterization, but it is true that what characterization exists in romance is far less psychological than modern readers, reared on the novel, expect. Henderson accordingly does much with Gavin's thoughts and personal history, including his sense of being "out of sorts."

A crucial symbol of both the mediaeval poem and *Sasquatch and the Green Sash* is the girdle or sash that the Gawain-character adopts near the climax of each narrative. In the mediaeval poem, as Gawayn prepares to face the Green Knight at the Green Chapel, a meeting where he expects to be decapitated, he successfully–and surprisingly, given his reputation as a ladies' man–avoids being seduced by his host's wife. He succumbs not to her offer of sex, but rather to a deception when she offers him a small love-token: a green sash or girdle, the real value of which resides not in its costly materials but rather that whoever wears it "my3t not be slayn"–cannot be killed (lines 1849-54). In the end, Gawayn is not beheaded, merely nicked in the neck; ironically, however, it is the very girdle meant to protect him that secures this nick.

In *Sasquatch and the Green Sash* this sash is described at one point by Henderson as "the *ceinture fléchée*, that métisse thing that interwove life's precious strands with such dignity and grace." At another, he refers to the sash as Gavin's "scarlet letter, but freshly green, not red!": an obvious allusion to the great American classic that Nathaniel Hawthorne (1804-64) himself labelled "a romance." The interweaving of different narrative and thematic strands is an important idea *in* Henderson's story, but it serves equally well as a closing comment *on* the story; for in the final analysis, Henderson retells a powerful tale with dignity and grace, successfully transplanting a poem rooted in the mediaeval Arthurian past into a particularly Canadian mythos.

FURTHER READING

The manuscript containing *Sir Gawain and the Green Knight* and the three other poems thought to be by the same author can be viewed online at http://contentdm.ucalgary.ca/digital/collection/gawain/.

The Arthur of the English: The Arthurian Legend in Medieval English Life and Literature. Ed. W. R. J. Barron. Cardiff: University of Wales Press, 1999.

Burrow, J. A. *A Reading of Sir Gawain and the Green Knight.* London: Routledge, 1965.

A Companion to the Gawain-Poet. Ed. Derek Brewer and Jonathan Gibson. Cambridge, UK: D. S. Brewer, 1997.

Cooper, Helen. *The English Romance in Time: Transforming Motifs from Geoffrey of Monmouth to the Death of Shakespeare.* Oxford: Oxford University Press, 2004.

Frye, Northrop. *Anatomy of Criticism: Four Essays.* Princeton: Princeton University Press, 1957.

—. *The Secular Scripture: A Study of the Structure of Romance.* Cambridge, MA: Harvard University Press, 1976.

Putter, Ad and Jane Gilbert, eds. *The Spirit of Medieval English Popular Romance.* Harlow: Longman, 2000.

Saunders, Corinne, ed. *A Companion to Romance: From Classical to Contemporary.* Oxford: Blackwell, 2004.

Sir Gawain and the Green Knight. Ed. J. R. R. Tolkien and E. V. Gordon. 2nd ed. Norman Davis. Oxford: Clarendon, 1967.

Sir Gawain and the Green Knight. [An original-language edition with facing-page translation]. Ed. and Trans. James Winny. Peterborough: Broadview, 1995.

Sir Gawain and the Green Knight. Trans. Marie Borroff. New York: Norton, 1967.

Stevens, John. *Medieval Romance: Themes and Approaches.* London: Hutchinson, 1973.

Whetter, K. S. *Understanding Genre and Medieval Romance.* Aldershot: Ashgate, 2008.

PART I

CHAPTER 1

Of all the high and mighty white men of the Northwest Territories, Arthur LeMagne was the greatest, so I've heard told, a French Canadian by birth, as the name suggests, born fifty-seven years previous, in the little Quebec town of Chamelot, but a Territories man for as long as anyone could remember, and certainly one of the richest – arctic diamonds primarily, though he was fascinated by oil and gas and northern peridot and was determined to make paying propositions of each. Arthur LeMagne loved holiday parties and would spare no expense. From the Winter Solstice to Christmas Eve, relatives and friends would be flown in to his favourite Mackenzie Mountain lodge, a vast log cabin castle, with roaring fires burning behind great stone hearths, wooden ceilings that gleamed in the firelight, and expansive views over Lake McTaggart and the Aurora Borealis that sometimes played over a ghostly, starlit sky fifteen hours for the keeping. Such was this night, a visual feast, cheek by jowl with a literal one, every colour of the rainbow spread across the firmament like God's Kandinsky, with the eeriest, fluorescent green predominant, and every local game meat on the table awaiting the delectation of his guests – blue goose and moose liver, bear steaks dripping with fat, and the finest cuts of bison and Dall sheep, a veritable *Ordre de Bon Temps*. Arthur LeMagne was in his element. Courses were piped in, for despite his French Canadian lineage, LeMagne loved haggis and pipes, Scottish regalia and Scots explorers, for this was the place of Alexander Mackenzie, "by land from Canada, July 22, 1793," of whose namesake river the Liard was the chief tributary.

LeMagne was proud of his guests. There at the head table sat Rupert Donovan of Gryphon Oil and Gas, President of Superior Drilling, Miroslav Kucharsky together with his lovely wife, May. Bustling, irrepressible, Bertha George, Chief Engineer of his own mines, sat right next to the head of the Yellowknife RCMP detachment, Phil Mattingly, in full red uniform. Phil's most promising recruit, Gavin McHenry, Arthur's favourite, not only because he'd discovered that he was in fact a distant cousin, but because he *chose* to come north when every other opportunity was open to him, Gavin, shy and unsure, was seated beside the most beautiful in all the west, LeMagne's very own Ghylaine, glinting and grey of eye, who talked to the young man and tried to make him feel at ease.

"Are you sad on Christmas Eve?" she asked. "Here. Help me pull this firecracker."

He did, smiled at the noise and the silly joke inside, and put up with her adjusting a pink party hat on his head.

"There," she declared. "Now you look better."

After prayers from Bishop Steinam, dressed in his finest beaded deerskin jacket, the glorious din resumed, laughter and tinkling of forks and knives, the clatter of trays, the pouring of wines and exchange of tales, not least of these, stories of a darkening world, for the Bishop was a man of the hour, well connected, and knew things others didn't. Talk turned to the wars in Levant, to the black banners of Jihad, the yellow of Shi'a and Hezbollah, portents of final days as foretold in Revelations and elsewhere, the destruction of the Jews and their one-eyed Deceiver, of the Infidels under their eighty flags, and the second coming of Christ, strange and extraordinary tales of the defeat of Rome at Dabiq near the border of Turkey, the ancient land of Byzantium. "Go to Sham," the prophet once declared, "and those who are not able to go to Sham should go to Yemen, for Al-Sham is the land of gathering for the Day of

Judgment. God chooses only the best to come, and they are known as strangers from foreign lands." Muhammad's words the Bishop quoted from the great compendium, the Book of Tribulations, and from the Koran.

Now Noah Poundmaker, grand Chief of the Dene nation, sat silent throughout, along with his sons, as did Gavin McHenry, though for different reasons. Sensing his distance, Ghylaine tried again, this time with Christmas trees. She nodded her head in the direction of three giant spruce at the end of the hall, profusely trimmed in white and scarlet and gold, bejeweled from top to bottom by lights twinkling on and off. Clothed in fresh needles, with their gummy sap and dark, pungent Christmas scent, from a time long back when there were no people at all, they stood, baubled and glimmering with as much art and colour as anyone could devise for such tall, spiky, primordial things. Ghylaine asked him if they were to his taste. "How could they not be?" he responded. They were better by far than the White House tree, taller by his reckoning than the President's.

"You know why there are lights on trees?" she asked, drawing him out.

"For Christ's sake, I imagine."

"Yes, of course, that, too. But not just. Arthur says they're for the solstice, you see, the shortest day of the year. Pagan tribesmen thought the sun and all its gold would disappear, so they brought the greenest winter thing they could find into the house and surrounded it with light. They wooed the sun, you might say, in its darkest hour, because they wanted it back. Isn't that a wonderful story?"

"So not Christian at all."

"No, no. I wouldn't say that. The missionaries didn't think that way. Probably, being diplomatic and good and proper missionaries, they did *not* say, 'How stupid of you, wicked barbarians, worshipping the sun. Stop it at once!' Probably they said, 'Splendid! Sunlight in the house, on the darkest day. And green things, too! But that's not only sunlight, you see. That is the eternal light of Jesus Christ, who died for our sins and who has promised you and your family not just rebirth, but perpetual life.'"

"A wonderful story. Good news and glad tidings, Madam LeMagne. Merry Christmas!"

Gavin McHenry raised his glass and smiled gallantly as he said the words, but his sadness soon returned, and since she was the wife of Arthur LeMagne and by reputation the loveliest woman in all the west, he was not about to tell her why. And when that clouded, slightly distracted look overcame him once again, and when he saw she seemed concerned, even peeved that he wouldn't explain himself, he said simply, "I'm sorry, Madam LeMagne. I'm a bit out of sorts, not fit for such a feast or for any good company at all," and promptly excused himself.

He took a turn in the frigid Arctic air. Even the slightest breeze bit into his cheeks, while the fluorescent green washed the heavens like a portent and seemed to exert a pressure on his shoulders and on the back of his neck, guiding him, involuntarily lightening him. He shook his head, as if to clear his mind, blew some misty breath into the cold, and clapped his mittened hands together. The snow squeaked beneath his boots. From a distance, he could hear a howling, wolves or dogs in town, he couldn't tell which, and when he clapped his hands together again, in a sudden swoosh, a snowy owl erupted in flight and soared into the night.

He returned inside, acknowledged the guests beside him, and right away heard the words, Robbie Burns, fully declaimed: "His knife see rustic Labour dicht.... And then, O what a glorious sicht, Warm-reekin, rich." They'd reached the stabbing of the haggis, a high moment for Arthur LeMagne, who loved all things from a bygone time, throwbacks, Nor'westers and Bay men, like the emperor of Rupert's Land,

George Simpson, Scotsmen, voyageurs, and native trappers, all those who thought nothing of distance and cold, who could paddle twenty hours at a stretch, sleep four, then repeat the performance. In the fire-lit warmth, the liquor flowed, foam-topped beer and bright wine. Then amid the laughter, clatter, and din, from the side porch door there hove into the hall, complete with traces and animals and sled, the most appalling figure, thickset, square, who in height outstripped all earthly men, his loins and limbs long and great, half a giant on earth, I do declare, though human for all that, and strangely handsome. At back and breast his body was broad, hips and haunches elegant, to say the least, all parts of the man perfectly proportioned—with one notable exception: feet like those no mortal had ever seen, like a snow-shoe hare's, though the size of a moose's, and worse, even more frightening, apart from his furious mien, a hue to cause both shock and awe, for the giant was coloured a gorgeous green.

All arrayed in green and gold was he, his body draped in a caribou coat, open at the front, trimmed on collar and sleeves with glorious amber spotted lynx, his parka the same, thrown back from his hair laid over his shoulders. Mukluks clung to his calves and gaped wide at the base, wider than ever men had seen before, and covered with quills and beads and embroidery of the most delicate kind, green always centered on gold. And gracing the fringe of his three-quarter coat, lapels and sleeves to boot, the greenest of arctic emeralds that ever glinted in fire-light, together with small gold bars aplenty, interspersed with carved peridot, butterflies, birds, and finest of all, twin mosquitoes in brooches, bravest near blood, fastened as tight as bugs could drink, each thorax red and fat as summer berries.

"Oh Mah," Chief Poundmaker said under his breath as he looked away at the floor.

"Nuk-luk," his son said, and frightened, looked to the same place.

The sled of this intruder was made of narwhal tusk, ivory, snow white and as precious as the Danish throne, runner tops, stanchions, bed slats, too, inset with gold and winking emeralds, sides fittingly clad in caribou hide, much like his coat, fringed with amber lynx and patterned with quills and beads, first green ones, then gold. Burnished bells hung tinkling down from traces, cleverly interwoven, that teamed not huskies or Siberians or Eskimo dogs, but four of the most gluttonous, tawny wolverines it was possible to imagine, with their playful, padded snow-shoe paws, *gula gula* to be sure, powerful snow-jumpers, most graceful when free, four of the sharpest-toothed weasels no wolves would meddle with, though they heeded their master's every look, even when loosed from their lines.

Gaily was that gargantuan man all geared in green, the weirdest St. Nicholas ever to step from a sleigh, the hair of his head like that of his beasts, fair flowing locks enfolding his shoulders. The beard that hung over his breast was as big as a bush, cut, together with the splendid strands that grew from his head, evenly all round above his elbows, a circle of golden hair like a king's hood guarding his neck like a lion's mane. Yet he carried no pistol, no Kalashnikov, no detonator, explosives, or grenades, but he held in one hand a holly branch, holly that is greenest when groves are gaunt and bare, and in the other a scimitar, graciously curved in the shape of a crescent moon, a sword suitable for Allah's work, I swear, or that of a sultan or the deadliest Ottoman Turk from olden days. By the hilt he brandished it, huge and monstrous; for it was a weapon fit for a fable, in length an ell or more, all cast in gold engraved steel and bejeweled with green gems, its blade burnished bright, honed acutely for cutting as the keenest razor. With enough tassels attached, each buttoned with pine green, richly embroidered, a rope hung from the pommel, swung in the same gracious curve over his shoulder, and hooked onto the scabbard.

Ignoring all peril, the giant strode through the hall, approached the head table, and greeting none, haughtily looked over their heads and asked, "Who is the governor of this merry gang? I'd gladly set eyes on him and reason with him for a while." He swaggered up and down before them, then paused, and waited to see who'd respond.

For the longest time Arthur's guests only stared at him, with his huge splayed feet, his look of summer lightning, and strokes swifter than a guillotine, for all marveled what it might mean that a man and his beasts should acquire such a hue, as to grow bright as dawn or green as grass and greener yet, it seemed, more gaudily glowing than green enamel on gold. They studied this alien thing, those nearest him trembling with amazement, all wondering what in the world he would do. The Northern lights may have seen queer sights, but never such a one; folks took it for fairy work, a dream figment, or apparition from a phantom world. Even the most forward held back, stifling themselves, and all sat stock-still, astounded by his speech, while a frozen, sleepy silence spread throughout the hall, like death or a grave beneath the snow.

CHAPTER 2

Arthur LeMagne had done a stint in the military, Black Watch, and was no coward. From the height of the small dais the owners of the lodge had built for the occasion, LeMagne thought he beheld the very spirit of adventure he'd come to love and admire. Courteously he greeted his gruesome guest and said, "Sir, you're in fact quite welcome here. I'm at the head of this table. My name is Arthur. I invite you to stay a while, and we'll learn later what you've come for."

"No, by heaven," said the man, "and by Him who sits there on such a special evening as this. My errand is not to spend time with you, but because your reputation is what it is and all your guests so highly regarded, honourable and courteous as may be, and because they hold to their word like a covenant, that's what made me wend my way here at so pointed an hour. You can be sure by this branch that I bear I pass in peace, seeking no plight whatever, for if I'd fared forth in fighting spirit, I've weapons and body armour enough at home, I assure you. As I'm waging no war, I wear softer clothes.

"Have patience with me, even if what I say may seem unjust. Under the archangel Gabriel's good guidance, I attend all men of the unseen, all those who seek truth, who honour their word, and for whom, as they say, quest outweighs request. I have given counsel to Moses, who led an entire people. With Alexander, the two-horned one, I've journeyed to the ends of the earth and seen the dark lands, in Siberia and under the Pole star, those of the Dene nation. Unbidden, I've discovered the river of eternal youth. This ivory sled you see, gleaming in firelight, comes from narwhal tusks, the horn of the ocean unicorn, given to

Charlemagne by the great Sultan Haroun-al-Rashid. All that I tell you can be verified.

"No, it's not fighting I seek, and I say this in good faith, since I see mostly beardless boys about anyway and other such redcoats and Crusaders that have cost truth dearly. I crave what you'd call a good Christian game, because it's Yuletide and New Year and a lot of charlatans and fake toughs are hanging about here. However, in this whole splendid dining hall, there may be one who holds himself in such high esteem, a keen one so headstrong he'd dare strike one stroke for another. If so, I'll make a gift of this curved blade, this sword, heavy enough, to handle just as he chooses. And I'll take the first blow as bare as I sit here. Anyone rash enough to try, step lightly toward me, latch onto this weapon – I quit any claim to it – keep it as your own. Stiff as a board, I'll stand your stroke, but only if after a year and a day's delay, you'll grant me the right to deal one back, unguarded and unchecked."

If he astonished them at first, stiller were the guests in that hall, from the high to the low. The horrid figure wrenched himself round, rolled his red eyes, knitted his brow, bristling green, busily waved his beard this way and that to see who might rise, and when no one would, coughed aloud and said, "What? This is Arthur's party, famous throughout the West? Where's your courage now and your great words? I let drop a whisper, and you're all shaking. Does no one here dare, or are all your detractors right? You fear the death they readily embrace. Therefore you can never triumph or know truth."

Then he laughed so loud, the blood shot for shame into young Gavin's face. He grew as wrathful as the wind and started slowly to rise when he heard his superior, Captain Mattingly call out, "This is absurd! What in heaven's name is in these drinks? And what madness is this you're asking? Give me that sword, for God's sake," and he reached for his revolver, but Chief Poundmaker laid a hand on his arm to quiet him and whispered, "This man is a sending from the spirit world. He takes a Sasquatch's shape and speaks your language. Do not disturb him."

Wider than a moose's, on his splayed, mukluked feet, like a snowshoe hare's, the apparition pulled himself up to his full height, by a head and more, higher than any in that whole hall, and with a stern glare stood there stroking his beard, and with a countenance as dry as the desert, undid his coat, no more dismayed or checkmated than if waiters had brought him a drink of whiskey. Quickly Gavin went to him where he stood fiercely on his feet, took the sword from his hand and swung it about, cutting the air with a whoosh, one for each rise and one for each fall.

"Take care with your cut, cousin," Arthur declared, "for what's at stake, and if you do it right, I dare say you'll bide your time for the return blow."

Scimitar in hand, Gavin went even nearer the monster of a man who, unblinking, awaited him. Without the slightest sign of alarm, the giant in green said, "Let's review our agreement before we go any further. State your name, I beg you. Tell it me truly, so I can trust your word."

"Gavin McHenry deals you this blow. Whatever happens thereafter, in twelvemonths' time, I'll take another, with whichever weapon you wish, and from no one else in this world."

The other answered again, "What a pleasure it is to bide a blow from you, Gavin. By God, I'm glad to get from your hand what I've called for. And with full true reason you've rehearsed the exact covenant I've demanded of you, except that you seek me out, wherever on earth you hope I can be found, and receive such wages as you pay me here before so splendid a gathering."

"How will I find you?" Gavin demanded. "Where is your place? As God gave me breath, I've no idea where you live, nor do I know, sir, your business or your name. Instruct me. Tell me what you're called.

I'll use all the wits I possess to wend my way wherever I must. You have my word on it, I swear. "

"That's New Year's resolution enough for me. I don't need more," said the man in green to Gavin, ever polite. "To tell you the truth, after you've smitten, my smooth one, and I've absorbed your blow, I'll be smart about it and tell you straightaway of my house and home and my own name. When you've kept to your covenant, then you can ask the way. And if I waste no words with you now, the better you can speed along, stay as long as you like in your own land, and seek no farther–But enough of this! Take hold of your grim tool, and let's see how well you swing."

"Gladly, indeed, sir," countered Gavin, stroking the steel for a bit.

On the ground the green man graciously stood, with head slightly slanting to expose the flesh. His long and lovely locks he laid over his head, neatly showing the naked neck, nape and all. Gavin gripped his sword and gathered it on high, looked at the monster beneath, then at the guests in the hall, and said, "To the hundreds, young and old, who leapt to a hideous death from the tops of high towers, each one falling and burning, to the schoolgirls disfigured by acid and shot in the head for the crime of learning, to the innocent, so-called unbelievers, raped, sodomized, and sold into slavery, to the unsuspecting youth, decapitated by a madman on a bus in Manitoba, or to all those Christians dressed in orange, beheaded on the beaches of Africa, I dedicate this blow and deliver it with the justice and vengeance of an angry God, who in his goodness, abhors atrocity almost as much as impunity."

Then Gavin set his left foot before him on the floor, brought the sword down swiftly on the bare flesh, so that the sharp blade sheared through, shattering the bone, sank deep in the sleek flesh, split it in two, and the tip of that scintillating steel bit into the floor. The fair head fell from its neck to the earth. As it rolled past, many guests kicked at it with their feet. Blood spurted from the body, scarlet against the green, yet that wild freak never faltered nor fell one whit, but on the strongest of Bigfoot shanks, stoutly sprang forward, there where head table guests stood in amazement. In a seeming rage, he reached out, roughly latched onto his lovely head, and straightway lifted it. Then he strode to his sled, and the wolverines bounded up to a large tinkling of bells like snow shook from their fur. He stepped onto the footboard, snatched at his whip, his other hand clutching his head by the hair. Headless, still he stood in his place, as if he'd suffered no injury at all, and turned his body round, that ugly trunk that bled. Many were seized with dread when they at last understood what he'd said.

For he held up the head in his hands even toward, for Arthur, the dearest one on that dais, turned its face, lifted its eyelids, looked glaringly, and mouthed this much, as here you can know: "Look, Gavin. You'd be wise to do as you've said and seek until you find, loyally, the way you should, as you've stated in this hall for all to hear. I charge that you chose to get at the Green Chapel just as good as you gave and that next New Year's morning you'll be duly made whole, as you deserve. Many men know me to be the keeper of that Chapel. Make an effort to find me, and you'll never fail. So come, or take your proper place as a coward."

Head in his hand, with a fierce tug at the traces, he hurtled out the hall door, snow flying up from the sled. To what kith he returned, no one knew; never the more were they aware from what country he'd come. What then? At that green thing, Arthur just laughed and grinned, whereas some in the room remarked on the marvels of science and wondered if what they'd seen had been staged. Poundmaker's son, Nelson, was dismayed by such talk and refused to hear of it. Though astonished at heart, Arthur let no semblance of that be seen but said outright, in a sly, measured speech to his companion, comely as ever:

"Dear lady, let nothing distress you today. Such strange events are fitting at Christmastime, little entertainments to make us laugh and sing, like Christmas carols. Nevertheless, I may just tuck in to this meat, since I've seen, I confess, a rare and extraordinary sight."

He glanced at Gavin and gamely said, "Now, sir, let's hang this sword up; it's done hewing enough." And it was hung above the fireplace, on a piece of velvet, where visitors could gaze in awe and by true title retell the wonder of it all. Then the guests walked toward a table, Arthur and his young cousin together, where dutiful folk served them double portions of dainty things. Amidst all manner of music and meats, they partied that night, well into the morning, too. "Now think carefully, Gavin," he heard himself say, "and don't blanch for pain at the cruel adventure you've taken in hand this day."

CHAPTER 3

Arthur may have grinned at the gruesome game played out at his party, but Gavin didn't. While others drank and danced and drank again, Gavin skipped only the dancing. He drew apart, half woozy and heavy-hearted, weighed down by his task. The Dene Chief's son, Nelson Poundmaker, saw him and went to sit beside him.

"You seem concerned, my friend. I've come to console you."

"Thank you. That's very kind. But I'm past hope for consolation."

"Why? Such spirits appear for a reason. Nuk-luk came because you have need of him."

"Have I? And why is that?"

"Only you can know. If you are troubled, state what troubles you. It will comfort you."

Some say beer unties the tongue; not so with Gavin McHenry. It merely made him retreat the more. But something about Nelson Poundmaker, perhaps the gentleness of his approach, or because he was native and knew things a young constable didn't, caused Gavin to warm to him.

"I had a girlfriend down south. Knew her for many years."

When he stopped short, Nelson Poundmaker asked, easing the way, "And she wanted to be with you?"

"Yes. She did. We had a child together. A boy."

"And where is this boy? With her?"

"No."

"With his grandparents?"

"No."

"Where then?"

"Nowhere."

The other young man looked at him intently. "Nowhere?"

"I made her get rid of it."

"Ah."

"You don't approve, I see."

"It's not for me to approve or disapprove."

"Maybe I'm the one who disapproves."

The young chief continued, "Your companion, she wanted this child?"

"Yes." And after a silence, Gavin added, "She'd even picked out a name. Christopher. She wanted to call him Christopher. 'There will be others,' I told her. 'Now is not the time.' And she believed me."

"But you don't think there will be others."

"No," said Gavin quietly. "No. It's finished."

"Ah. And now you have this bad story you must live through – if you can survive it."

"I don't see how," Gavin said, reflecting on his fate. "I've given my word, and I don't see how."

"You have a bad story to live, but you have no son." Nelson Poundmaker looked away, then added, "Stories are not worth sons."

Before he left him, the Dene Chief's eldest said, "I will help you. My father and I will prepare you for this journey. Whether you survive or die, it is better to be ready."

Soon the year slid past, never the same twice, as forming and finishing seldom accord. So that Yuletide yielded itself over, and the year after that; season after season in succession went by. After Christmas comes the crabbed Lenten time, that forces on true believers' flesh fish and foods yet simpler. Then the world's weather wars with winter. Cold ebbs and declines; clouds lift, descend again, and by early May in the northern Nahanni, cool showers are shed, falling upon lichen and spindly spruce, on rock and turlough and karst, gray granite canyons in endless pursuit, where streams swallow themselves into the earth, course miles underground, through caves and caverns, through cenotes and sinkholes, then gather themselves in turquoise watered lakes, death lakes that rise and fall in huge granite tubs, imprisoned, for God gave them no outlet at all.

Then flowers begin to show, fireweed, alpine anemone, wild arctic rose; grounds and birch groves alike are garbed in green. Birds begin to build and brightly sing for solace of the ensuing summer, and boreal forests teem with sunlight making the most of its brief stay and lasting the whole day long. From kingfisher, rock ptarmigan, from sandhill crane, calls and songs echo forth across the rock-filled plains. Magic ovals and circles decorate this northern land, interlink one with another; in secret hollows, nests, and caves, in birds' eggs and in the bellies of foxes, field mice, and bears, small heads grow and acquire their features, fleeting as a gust of wind.

During that short season of summer, when Zephyrus himself seems to blow on seeds and herbs and pollen fills the moist air, mitreworts wax full in yellow-green splendor. A dunking of dew drops from their leaves, as they bide the blush of an endless sun, and the tiniest vampires begin to take flight, mosquitoes, black flies, blood-born, tormenting birds and bears alike, sawing at the thinnest flesh of nostrils and ear-lobes, then sipping their red drink, and driving the Dene women harvesting birch bark to wear bee-bonnets even in June.

Then August comes hurrying, urging plants on, warning them because of winter to wax ripe soon. Cold gusts bring September flakes that fly up from the face of the rock strewn earth. Wrathful winds in raging skies wrestle with the sun. Leaves are lashed loose from the trees, lie on the ground, and the grass becomes gray that was green before. What rose from root now ripens and rots. So the year in passing yields its many yesterdays, and winter soon wends its way again, as the world demands, I swear. The people's river, the great Nahanni, begins to freeze, and on Michaelmas moon, Nelson Poundmaker comes bearing bannock and blackberry pie to guard, like the archangel, against the dark of night, for now is the autumn equinox, daylight visibly shorter, and Gavin busies himself with thoughts of his anxious plight.

PART II

CHAPTER 4

On All Saints Day, November first, Nelson Poundmaker invited Gavin McHenry to the Nahanni Butte council headquarters of the Dene people. There various chiefs had convened, Eric Etchinelle, Dodinal Laboucan of the Behdi Ahda first nation, Belvidere Jumbo and Bors Bonnetrouge, both strong men, Lionel Arrowmaker of the local band, together with Jean Marie Mador, much admired. There was drum dancing, in which Gavin was asked to take part.

"If we sing well," Nelson Poundmaker said, "it will shorten your journey."

Already the ground had frozen deeply. Snow covered the bush, and ice squeezed the streams on both sides into dark narrow strings. Afterwards that night, many chiefs commiserated with the young man and gave him advice. He must travel by dogsled and snowshoe. There could be no question of skidoo. All forest creatures were frightened by skidoos. His dogs must be trained dogs, quiet, obedient, brave, not spooked by caverns or caves, for legend had it Nuk-luk inhabited Nahanni caves, and McHenry would have to seek him there. In that strange place the green chapel most likely lay, in caves fronted during summertime by green porches, where Dall ewes nursed their young and sought shelter from storms. No one knew for sure, because locals did not venture there, in Mackenzie Mountain heights where wild men lived and intruders often died, many discovered later, headless.

"Do you have your captain's blessing?" Nelson Poundmaker asked.

"Yes and no," Gavin answered. "I told him whatever that creature might be, it threatened the peace and order of the territory and spread terror wherever it went, as did others of like mind. He agreed but said I must take a leave of absence to do what I had to do. I shouldn't implicate the Royal Canadian Mounted Police in any way whatever, since what I did was entirely of a personal nature."

"You don't share this view?"

"No. Absolutely I do not. How can the war against such frightful things be entirely of a personal nature?"

"'Render unto Caesar the things which are Caesar's. Render unto God the things that are God's.' That's what your people say. If you approach your journey with humility, you won't make a mistake. Tomorrow I'll dress you. My brothers, my father and I will wish you good-bye and god speed. Now you must speak to the leaders of the people who are gathered together waiting to hear what you have to say."

Gavin could tell they grieved for him; nevertheless, they made light of his troubles and gently joked about his plight. He spoke to them sorrowfully of his departure then pertly said, "Honoured chiefs, now I beg my leave of you. You know the cost of the case. I won't waste breath on trivial things, but I'm bound to bear my blow and must be gone tomorrow to seek the man in green. God will guide me."

All applauded his pluck and promised their prayers were with him.

Gavin stayed there that day, and at dawn on the morrow, Nelson Poundmaker and his brothers laid out his garments. First a splendid carpet they rolled out over the floor, a lovely tree of life, delicately woven in blues and reds, corn stalks rooted in the earth, tassels, each seed tessellated with its sister, reaching far into the sky. Corn leaves were laddered like the stages of creation, and from each rose birds and butterflies, conversing as if in the green language of god. Shaking his head in wonder, Gavin asked about its origin.

"Some say they were once the saddle pads of Turkish warriors," Poundmaker declared. "Others say they came via Toledo and the Arab centers of Spain. This one is a gift from our southern cousins. Navajo and Dene speak the same tongue and can converse with one another. Some of our legends we share."

Spread out on the carpet were the garments Gavin was asked to wear.

"You must go on your journey prepared," Nelson Poundmaker said. "These clothes will do Nuk-luk justice. Many of our people have forgotten the skills, but some haven't."

Here skills encompassed an elegant geometry of circles and bars in soft greens and reds and blacks, painted up sleeves and across shoulders of a winter coat as stunning as any Andalusian holy place. Mukluks and mittens were made to match, a parka edged with ermine, beaded and quilled with preening eaglets, appearing at intervals, and beaver kit tails tied by true-love-knots traced as thickly as if a score of maidens had been stitching them seven winters long.

"You can hunt with no rifle," young Poundmaker warned, "but must use something silent and deadly." He showed him a crossbow, skillfully made, stock and stirrup and string all cleverly interlinked, with a telescope sight to make sure of its strike. "The park is small. If we have our way, no white man will hunt in the whole watershed. Sleep on spruce boughs," he added, "and go as quietly as the breeze. These, too, will help as the snow thickens."

He pointed to a pair of snowshoes, and Gavin thanked him profusely for his help, then asked about other shared legends he might know.

"Dene and Navajo don't share this legend," he said, "but I like it. It's the story of Changing Woman. In the spring she's young and beautiful. In the fall and winter she's old. Her dances on mountaintops created jewels and clothing, animals and plants. When she becomes too old she walks toward the east, meets her younger self, merges with her, and becomes young again. She's the giver of many blessings, and her son slew the monsters that beset his people. If on your journey you chance to meet Changing Woman and receive a gift from her, you can consider it an honour."

Gavin McHenry fell silent as he contemplated what his friend had just told him and what it might mean. Then Poundmaker asked, "Have you no totem?"

"Totem?"

"Something your father has given to protect you."

Gavin thought a moment, was about to shrug and dismiss the question, when suddenly it occurred to him.

"Perhaps I do," he said.

He reached into his pocket and took out his keychain. Attached was a plastic tag, green Scotch plaid background, upon it a pentangle surmounted by a golden crescent moon; underneath the words read, "*Solus virtus nobilitat.* Virtue alone ennobles"–the clan crest, a gift from his father.

"Good," Poundmaker said. "You suit it well."

And though I digress, I intend to tell you why the crescent moon and pentangle is proper to this young member of the Royal Canadian Mounted Police. It is a symbol Solomon once conceived to betoken holy truth, which it is entitled to do, for it is a figure that has five points, and each line overlaps and is locked with another. It is endless everywhere, and the English call it, as I've heard, the Endless Knot. Therefore, it goes with Gavin and his winter gear, protection against the cold, for, ever faithful in five things, each in fivefold manner, he strove to be known for good, devoid of sin, like virtue's gold, well-refined. First he sought to be faultless in his five senses, including the sixth, which like his five fingers never failed him. Then he sought to fix the body's five cardinal points, four limbs plus guiding head, the moral compass of his mortal life. Five continents in this world contain the forms of holy truth, in all their varied guises, three Abrahamic faiths, two testaments, both old and new, the sum of which comes down to us in the five wounds of Christ, the five pillars of Islam, and the five smooth stones David used to slay Goliath. Five primary colours, I might add, mark the battlefields of Judgment Day, the black of Jihad, yellow of Hezbollah, the green of Al Khidr, Satan's red, cleansed by Jesus' blood, and the snow white of Mary, queen of heaven, whose virgin birth redeemed the world, for Gavin's mother was also named Mary.

The fifth five I find Gavin practiced were these: frankness and fellowship above all things, his courtesy and cleanness of spirit, never crooked or bent, and past all points, compassion; these pure five were more firmly affixed to that fine young man than to any other. Truly, all five were conferred on Gavin, each one locked to the other, so that none had an end, fastened in five points which never failed, neither assembling on one side nor sundering either, without end at any nook or corner I can find anywhere, wherever the design began or came to its finish. That is the pure pentangle according to the people's lore.

And what of the crescent moon? Some said it stood for Hecate and all such liminal places on the Bosphorus, portals from one state to another–she whose moonlight saved Byzantium from Philip of Macedon, though, a full millennium later, not from Sultan Mehmed. Others claimed Turkish conquerors fell in love with her, kept Hecate's moon for themselves, and displayed it jealously on their banners. Others still said the crescent was in fact the woman of the apocalypse, the Virgin herself, as portent of Judgment Day, conqueror of the New World, like Mary of Guadeloupe standing on a silver moon in Mexico. What roundabout way a pentangle and a crescent moon could reach the hills of Scotland, no one was quite able to say, least of all Gavin, yet there it stood on his keychain, in gold and plain green plaid, a clan crest in the northern lands of Canada.

CHAPTER 5

Captain Philip Mattingly was sick at heart that Gavin felt so compelled to honour his commitment. He'd said to him, softly, like a father to his son, that he had a glowing future ahead of him and that he had no need to seek out his own destruction, to be utterly destroyed, beheaded by so arrogant an unearthly being.

"I've never seen such nonsense! Who'd believe that Arthur LeMagne could treat you so capriciously? Christ, it's an evil thing that a fine young man like you, full of life and promise, should be lost to us. You could have been chief here, had you shown more caution."

Was that a tear Captain Mattingly wiped from his eyes? It was indeed, so the story goes. But he couldn't just bid good-bye to his protégé without a parting gift – six of the finest Eskimo dogs, quiet, primed to hold off much larger prey, even polar bears. Gavin's team, along with a sled fully packed, were ready to load into the Cessna plane for the flight from Fort Simpson to Nahanni Butte, where the Nahanni River joins the Liard and all technology would be abandoned. Even young Poundmaker approved when he first saw the dogs, put his hand on the heart of the leader, and looked up toward his friend.

"These are athletes," he said with a smile in his eye. "The heart beat is slow and steady, like good drumming. They are sound dogs and will take you far, if you treat them well. Here," he added. "Spruce gum should you injure yourself. And here. Beaver fat. Take it for indigestion. Use the sulfur streams upriver in cold weather. They are magic places. And remember to find the Green Chapel in highland caves. I can't tell you not to fear them, for I know what you seek, but they give shelter to sheep, so perhaps to lost sheep like yourself, as well."

Gavin embraced his friend and bade him good-bye, then called out "Mush" to his team. Peowish, the leader, who'd had his tongue bitten off in a fight, sullen but fiercely loyal, dug hard at the traces, and they set off for this northern land before time, no comrades but for his dogs, no food that he cared for despite the provisions, and no traveler to talk to on the trail but God. Deadman Valley, which the Dene call Daktaehth', he kept always on his left, and in bone chilling cold that cracked the trees like cannon fire, he fared past outcroppings of rock as large as the castles of Wales, toward the wilderness of Death Lake, where dwelt few beloved by either God or good-hearted men. And always as he went, he asked whomever he met, trapper and native alike, if they'd heard anyone speak of a green giant or of a green chapel in any cave or remote place round about. And they all looked at him askance and said no, that never in their lives had they seen a man who bore such a colour of green.

His way was wild and strange, through canyons miles in length, sheer precipice stone, heaving up a thousand feet on either side, hewn by what glacial axe no man could say, nor for what purpose–gorges so jagged and deep, crevices so perilous and sudden in the snow, he thought them a mad god's surgery, incisions, random and brutal, performed in blood-less rage against the innocent earth. And always Gavin bore north, searching for what Captain Mattingly had told him could be found there among the darkest and narrowest of cuts, fearsome, unexplored, the canyon freakishly named Scimitar.

Like an alien thing, he travelled far from his friends, climbed over cliffs, and looked out right and left for caves, signs, and predators; grizzly bears were hibernating, so the worst he was spared, but once on a trail, remote and not usually trapped, in deep snow Gavin was tamping down with his snowshoes for the dogs, he heard a desperate snarling and clattering. Round the bend came a wolverine dragging a trap, who saw this human and came towards him with a look of such ferocity Gavin had never before seen in an animal's face. He reached for his crossbow, fired, and wounded the beast, but it merely redoubled its efforts, madder and more active than before, held as it was by only one claw of one hind foot. Gavin found time to fire again. The beast fell dead, and Gavin fed its carcase to the dogs, this wild and primitive thing that ran with mastodons and three-toed horses and half-refused to die. Ever after he felt spied upon, always in the vision of foes–prey, both dogs and human alike, for wolves whose howlings the dogs imitated on cold, star-lit nights, or worse, for long lost Naha tribesmen, those of beheading tales, who Dene legend says disappeared from the face of the earth a century before and were never heard from again

Yet the threats did not faze him; worse was the winter, when cold, fat flakes descended from the clouds and gathered, whipped by wind, in thick banks. Half slain by blizzard, night after night among the naked rocks, he slept on black spruce boughs, while Peowish and his team dug themselves deep in the snow. Warm sulfur springs bubbled up from the earth, and fresh ones hung high over his head in hard icicles. So in peril, hardship, and pain, Gavin traversed that country alone till Christmas Eve, then prayed to the Virgin and to his mother, her namesake, as ancestor and protector, that he might be shown some shelter, some mercy and warmth.

Lying too near a sulfur stream would deprive him of sleep, Gavin thought, but on the contrary, he awoke refreshed and almost merry that morning, fed the dogs and himself, then made his way up a steep incline. They toiled all the brief daylight long. On the few bare twigs of stunted spruce that clung to the stones, birds in misery piped piteously away, pining from cold. Gavin dreamed of Christmas Mass, in service of Him who that same night was born of a virgin to be victor over our

strife. Then toward twilight, at four p.m. that northern winter solstice, only a few short years ago, beneath a shallow moon that shone down on the mouth of a cave, he spied the form of a Dall sheep ram with its huge curved horns, more bone weight there than in the rest of its body combined, proof, if ever need be in this wild land, of the paramountcy of head butting and of rutting, the crack of bone on bone echoing across mountain redoubts, harbinger of lambs to come.

The dogs at first would not enter, fearing the darkness, but Gavin had a flashlight, a concession to his own time. Peowish whined, but went forward. In a broad gallery deep within, stalagmites like witches' fingers pointed toward an absent sky, and in a chamber off to one side, down a steep embankment even such strong and nimble beasts could not climb, dozens of horned sheep skulls lay spread across the earth. Above, as if in commemoration, inset and interlinked, ice crystals, blue and winking in Gavin's flashlight, like giant arctic diamonds, decorated this dome of the chapel of death.

Deeper still, the passage narrowed until it seemed impossible for the sled to pass, yet the dogs were not in the least discouraged, pulled even harder, and barked excitedly, Peowish nipping at the haunches of those he felt weren't doing enough. Finally, by tilting the sled on an angle, they fought their way through, and sensing what seemed to be moonlight in the distance, they strained and pulled and quickened their pace till Gavin felt first the cold, dank air replaced by breezes warm and infinitely sweeter, then saw the opening more clearly than ever before. Once there, below them spread out a valley of extraordinary beauty and peace. The moonlight turned the surrounding snow-capped peaks silver but cast itself down on a snowless earth, filled with trees and verdant growth and fields of seven foot tall timothy – a suntrap for sure, where the only wind that blew was a warm southwest Chinook, and it blew all the time, softly through mountain passes bringing nothing but a gentle rain.

Hardly had he crossed himself before Gavin McHenry caught sight through the trees of a lodge made of logs, well-lit, yellow-orange against the circling green, the comeliest structure he could possibly conceive, placed in an impregnable palisade of pointed stakes, on a plain with a handsome park of aspen and birch all around. He contemplated this wonderful gift from heaven, heaved off his parka, and heartily thanked Jesus and Julian, patron saint of travelers, kindly both, who had so courteously granted his prayer. *"Un bon hôtel,"* he said to himself, *en français* for effect. "I pray I'm welcome here." Then he urged Peowish forward and by good chance happened upon the main path, down which clattered dogs and man and sleigh. The door was unlocked, thick and solidly built, like the walls, well chinked, through which no harsh arctic wind could ever make its way.

CHAPTER 6

So many pale stone chimneys sprouted from the roof, so many white crocheted curtains hung from the windows, so many neat gables angled down to verandahs and decks, that large as it was, it seemed pure and pared out of paper, like a small boy's first snowflake pinned to the schoolroom window. To Gavin McHenry it would be good enough, if he could gain entrance, sojourn in that great house, and relax a little, at least while the holiday lasted. He knocked at the door, and soon a porter appeared, pleasant indeed, who greeted the wanderer and seemed prepared to answer every question.

"My good man," said Gavin, "Would you carry my message to the owner of this place, that I would truly appreciate a bed for the night?"

"Of course," the porter replied. "You'd be welcome to stay as long as you like, I do believe."

Then away he went and quickly returned with a throng of well-wishers ready to do him every conceivable service. They cared for his dogs, unpacked and housed his sled, escorted him into a large lounge with chairs everywhere, from which rose all sorts of guests, chattering and excited, eager to meet him, as if he'd been long expected, like a truant movie star. When Gavin removed his parka, several jumped forward to receive it, his mittens too. Many people, some in native dress, pressed in to greet him, to shake his hand, pay their respects, or have their picture taken near him, still in his mukluks. They brought him into a hall where a blazing fire lay fiercely burning. Then the head of that band came down from his room, to show Gavin deference and meet with him below. He said, "Make yourself at home. Do as you please with everything here. All is your own, at your own will and pleasure."

Astonished at this reception, Gavin declared, "I'm overwhelmed! You're so kind, you bring a tear to a fellow's eye," and the two, quite moved, clasped each other in a warm embrace.

Gavin gazed at the man who'd greeted him in so goodly a way and thought the place possessed a powerful chieftain, huge, in the prime of his life, with broad cheekbones and a peerless complexion, all beaver-hued. Stern of temper, limbs stalwart and strong, face as fierce as the fire, free in his speech, he seemed well suited, so Gavin felt, to lead such a company of fine, upstanding folk. This striking figure was imprinted on Gavin's thoughts almost forever, as happens at times to those barely out of their teens. Nor was that the only thing that pierced the young man's memory. Opulent and cultured as any Arthur LeMagne could lay claim to, this was a place brimming over with language, English, French, Dene, that mystical, incantatory thing, musical, almost sing-song, strange with its exploding "k's" and agglutinative syllables, ancient as Welsh or Arabic or Anglo-Saxon and as difficult to grasp, or so Nelson Poundmaker had informed him. To the English mind, everything in Dene was reversed, runic, complex. There was no phrase for "I love you." Instead, a Dene hunter would have to say *neranyenirstran*, "toward you my mind is habitually drawn."

Then the Chief led him to a hallway and expressly commanded that chambermaids be assigned to care for him. At his bidding attendants stood ready, who brought him to a beautiful bedroom, fit for a prince–for this was no ordinary place. The Dene chief had not thrown away his watch, as Gavin had heard told in some stories; nor did people work only when they wanted to. In that special hybrid place, eclectic, backward looking, bed curtains of brilliant silk with golden hems sported elaborate coverlets each with comely panels, bright ermine on top and embroidered all round with Dene flowers and animals—a curious mix. The crocheted curtains ran on cords with red gold rings; tapestries from Turkey and Persia hung tight to the walls, the same spread out on the floor underfoot. There with teasing remarks he was stripped of his warm winter clothes. Valets readily brought him jackets of the supplest caribou hide, moccasins to match, skillfully circled and sewn with rainbows of wildflowers, centered by little silver studs. And as soon as he chose and changed, to well nigh everyone there, truly it seemed from his looks that spring had come in all its colours. Beneath the clothes, Gavin's limbs, so lithe and glowing with life, convinced them all that Christ never had made so handsome and youthful an officer.

At a chimney hearth where charcoal glowed, a chair was placed with quilted cushions, delicately worked. Then a magnificent Pendleton coat of many colours, fur-lined with lynx and rabbit, surpassing that of Chief Joseph of the Nez Percés himself, was cast over Gavin's shoulders, maroon in hue but interspersed with oranges, greens, and cobalt blues in long trailing lines of patterns and shapes, intricate as any Alhambra mosque. Richly attired, he sat in that chair, warmed himself, and mended his good humour. Might this be how God revealed Himself, he wondered. In a garden, a well-appointed room, or a kaleidoscope of riotous colour? The best to be achieved was only intimation, he felt certain, accompanied by fellowship that mended good humour and asked to think of each thing well.

Soon a huge trestle table was covered with a thick tablecloth, brilliantly white and set with silver spoons, saltcellars, and napkins. When he was ready, Gavin washed and went to his meal. Cordially, men served him, soups and stews, lavishly seasoned, double helpings of fish of all kinds, grilled Arctic grayling, caught in river weirs, whitefish from local lakes and baked in pastry, boiled carp, pike flavoured in spices, always accompanied by the subtlest of sauces that Gavin judged irresistible. Waiters politely prodded him to eat more. "This is just penance food. We'll make amends soon." Gavin grew mirthful and full of good cheer, for the wine had already gone to his head. "If this is penance," he said, "What is heaven?"

Then he felt himself spied out, subtly encouraged by deft questioning to reveal that he was indeed an officer of the crown, straight from Fort Simpson, that it was in fact Gavin McHenry himself who sat there among them, come that Christmas, as chance would have it. And when the chief in that hall learned what man he had in his house, he laughed out loud, so pleased was he with the thought. And all his guests laughed too, sang Gavin's praises, and made it seem his name was attached to nothing but fame and glory. One lady drew near her neighbour and with a twinkle in her eye remarked, "This is the one whose reputation rates first in the ranks of men," to which her friend replied, "Now we'll observe the seemliest of manners and learn all the terms of talking 'noble,' unteachable by half, of course." A third laughed, "God has been gracious to us. Have we not fallen upon the fine father of nurture himself?" And smiles broke out all round that table, as the first returned to the fray. "Ladies, he's an expert. If we listen closely, wayward as we are, I'm sure we'll learn everything there is to know about love."

When dinner was done and Gavin got up, it was almost midnight. A pair of priests made their way to a chapel where small bells rang for midnight mass, as rightly they should at so holy a time. The chieftain was moved to prayer, his lady too; into her private pew she prettily walked. Gavin quickly advanced to go there too, but the Chief seized his sleeve and guided him to his seat, acknowledged him by name, and in his well-bred way, assured him he was the welcomest man in the world. He thanked him heartily; each embraced the other and sat soberly the whole service through.

The lady was then inclined to have a better look at this young man. Together with a bevy of beautiful women, she abandoned her pew. Fairest of all was she, in her body, her cheeks, her face, in complexion, features, and bearing, fairer than even Ghylaine, the loveliest in all the west, or so Gavin once thought. Courteously, she came through the chancel to greet him, another lady leading her by the left hand, a woman much older than she, almost ancient it seemed, highly honoured by all the guests about. Unlike to look upon those ladies were, for if the young was fit, yellowed was the other. Hues rich and rubious were arrayed on the one; rough wrinkled cheeks rolled downward on the other. On the one, kerchiefs with many clear pearls set off her breast and bright throat, bare to the sight, tawny and fragrant as the scent of winter cedar. The other was swathed in a choker that covered her neck, her swarthy chin wrapped in dark coloured veils, her forehead enfolded in cloth, muffled up everywhere, trellised round with feathers, trefoils, and tiny rings, like an old-style squaw or Muslim matron. Nothing was bare on that dame but her black brows, two eyes, and naked lips, and those were a sorry sight, chapped and bleared. A venerable woman indeed, men may call her, in God's name. Her body was squat and thick, her buttocks bulging and broad. Like liquorish for looking was the sweet one by her side.

CHAPTER 7

Gavin glanced at that beauty, who gave him a kind look, and with a nod from the Chief, he approached them again. The elder he saluted, then took the lovelier one a little in his arms and complimenting her, kissed her on both cheeks, the way the French do. They asked that they get to know one another better, and he quickly offered whatever services they might need, should it please them. Then they took him between them and, in close conversation, led him to a room, to a fireplace, and called for spice cakes, which chambermaids speedily brought, together with the finest of single malt whiskey. Often the Chief would jump up from his seat, so excited was he, and insist on merry-making that Christmas and New Year season. On a quiver of hunting arrows standing nearby, hung a gorgeously sewn parka and with laughing words he declared, "I promise you. Before I lose this parka, here with the help of my good friends, I intend to compete with the best!"

"Ink'on!" Gavin heard. *"Ink'on!"* And when he asked what that meant, he was told, "Medicine power!" A gracious guest explained why. Before their chief, eight men on their haunches lined up in a row, each with a dollar in his hand. When the drums began to beat, hands beneath jackets or parkas, they all concealed their tokens, some perfecting the concealment by inserting their thumbs behind their fingers. The drumbeats increased and the crouching men bobbed and swayed and weaved, sometimes jerking in time to the rhythm, sometimes chanting, stretching arms out from their torsos or waving them all about, rolling their eyes heavenward or, trance-like, closing them entirely, while the Chief, as captain of the opposing team, clapped loudly to guess which hand

contained the hidden coin. When he guessed right, that was *Ink'on*, medicine power; his opponent was killed and had to drop out of the line. When he guessed wrong, that was not *Ink'on*, and amidst laughter and shouts from his rivals, an arrow was piled up at the side of the room. Then the ones that remained re-hid their coins, trying their best to outwit their Chief. The drumming grew louder, the bobbing and weaving and folding of arms more frenetic still, until at the crescendo of this guessing game, only one survivor left, it was loudest of all, pounding, driving, "to make him smart," as Gavin's friend declared.

"The Chief is good," he went on to add, in a loud whisper over the sound of the drums. "You cannot fool him. He remembers players' patterns, *idzi* patterns, we say, who does what when, and his claps kill many players, even in the first round." Then he paused a moment. "Except in *naidah*. In *naidah* he isn't so good."

"*Naidah?*" Gavin asked.

"When the killed ones are raised from the dead. They get another chance. Good for Christmastime, eh? Then the Chief is not so good. No one knows why. He doesn't guess right and kill them again, the way he should. So we argue with him to step down and let another guesser take *naidah*. That way we are sure to win." So Gavin was kept amused with games in that hall that night, until it was so late the Chief ordered lights out, and Gavin took his leave and went to bed.

In the morning, as men mind the time our lord was born for our own destined death, good cheer for his sake wells up throughout the world in each and every one. So did it there in the far north of Canada on that day, by means of exquisite delights, daintily prepared, both light meals and formal dinners, served at that dais in remote Mackenzie Mountains by strapping young lads, flowered and costumed in the best Dene manner. The old ancient wife sat highest in honour, the Chief, so I'm told, politely beside. Gavin and the pretty one sat together, mid-table, as the first dishes were served, then next, the whole hall, all according to station. There was meat; there was mirth, so much joy everywhere that it pains me to tell of it, especially if I tried to pinpoint every detail. Yet this much I know. Gavin and that beautiful woman found such comfort in each other's company, through their playful flirtations and private remarks, their chaste and courteous exchanges, entirely free from the filth and dirty talk so prevalent these days, that you may take it for certain their word-play surpassed all other amusements on Christmas day. Since such winter festivities came via the Scots, piping burst forth, as each man tended to his pleasure, and the pair tended to theirs.

Much merriment was made that day, and on the morrow again, and like wild geese, it thronged in once more the third day thereafter; gentle on the ears were the joys of St. John's Day, the final feast, so folks there did think. But some guests were ready to go in the morning, so they forced themselves to stay awake and drank whiskey, drummed and danced and chanted the whole night through. Then at last, when it was very early, they took their leave, each on strange paths Gavin could barely discern. He himself said good-bye to his host, who grasped his arm, led him to his own room, and beside the fire, detained him, thanking him dearly for the fine favour he'd bestowed on them by honouring his house on that high occasion and embellishing the place with his sparkling good humour.

"I tell you, young man, as long as I live, I'll be the better that Gavin McHenry of the RCMP was my guest at Great Spirit's own feast."

"Merci, monsieur," said Gavin gravely. "Really it's all yours; all the pride of place is your own, sir, and may Mother Mary on high repay you. I'm at your service to do whatever you request. I'm honour bound by that, by every right, in small things and large."

The Chief took real pains to hold Gavin longer, but the young man replied there was no way that could happen. Then frankly, but courteously, that brusque man inquired of him what grim deed at so festive a time might drive him from a Chief's hall into a world of solitary woe, even before the holidays had ended.

"Really, sir," the young officer replied, "You're saying nothing but the truth. An important mission, not to say urgent, a debt superseding all others requires me to part from you, for I myself am summoned to seek out a place for which I have no idea in the world where to look. And so help me God, for all the land in the north, I can't fail to find it by New Year's Day. That's why, sir, I am making this one request, that you tell me, in all honesty, if you've ever heard tales of a green chapel, on what ground it might stand, and who the man is, the colour of green, who keeps it—a Sasquatch.... Nuk-luk, I'm told. You may have seen his prints in the snow on mountain peaks, or in the mud beside rivers or streams. He harks back to ancient days I'm told, to lost tribes long gone. A solemn pact was sworn between us that if I lasted, I meet that man at the green chapel, on the spot. This same New Year's is just about here; God willing, by His Own Son, I'd look that monster in the eye more gladly than I'd win the lottery. That's why, if you'll allow me, I must be on my way. I have only three days to get my business done, and I'd rather fall down dead than fail in my duty."

Then the Chief laughed, "Now you *must* stay, for I'm going to direct you to your meeting in good time. As for the whereabouts of the green chapel, stop worrying. You'll be in your bed, my brave man, at your ease for half the day, fare forth only on the first of the year, and reach that place by mid-morning, to do what you must. Stay here till New Year's Day, rise, and leave then. Someone will set you on your path. It's not two miles from here."

Then Gavin, fully gratified, gamely laughed, "Thank you so very much for this, above everything else. My objective's achieved. And at your will, I *shall* stay—and do whatever you deem appropriate."

Then the Chief seized him and sat him down beside him and let the ladies be fetched, all the more to please him, and privately among them all there flowed a quiet kind of solace. Suddenly the Chief, like one beside himself with joy, let fly words so ecstatic he seemed hardly to know what he said. Crying aloud, he declared to his young guest, "You've pledged to do the deed I ask! Right here and now, will you hold to this vow?"

"Yes, of course, sir," said the officer of the crown. "While I'm under your roof, I'm bound to do your bidding."

"You've travelled far," said the Chief, "and stayed up late. You're well stocked with neither food nor sleep, that much I know. So. You're going to lounge in your bed, sleep in at your leisure tomorrow morning until mass, then breakfast whenever you like–with my wife, who'll sit with you, comfort you with her company, until I return to the lodge. You stay, and I'll rise early to go hunting."

With a nod of his head, Gavin agreed to all this, as a good officer should.

"What's more," said the Chief, "let's make this bargain. Whatever I win in the woods you profit by, and what luck you have here we exchange. Let's swap so, my dear man. Swear to me you'll do it, for better or worse."

"By God," said the young officer, "I'm up for that. And may I add how much I appreciate your sporting inclinations."

"Someone bring us a drink. Then we've got ourselves a bargain!" the leader of the band declared. And they all burst out laughing.

They drank single malt whiskey, dilly-dallied, engaged in light-hearted conversation, both men and women alike, for as long as they pleased. Then with lovely French phrases and manners, learned from when long ago, they stood, softly speaking, kissed each other on both cheeks, and took their leave. By many brisk porters, down hallways gleaming with light, each man was escorted to a downy soft bed. But before retiring, again and again, they repeated the bargain. That old band Chief really knew how to have fun!

PART III

CHAPTER 8

Early before the break of day folks arose. Those guests preparing to go packed their bags and readied dogs and sleds, for beyond the suntrap, not far up the wooded mountain slopes, the snow was deep and the cold intense. They lined the dogs in their traces and seized their whips, each man taking the path he preferred. Nor was that well-loved Chief the last to get up. He ate a hasty breakfast, and with a dozen or so of his men, made for the forest to bow-hunt wood caribou.

In the thick of the trees, by a frozen lake, they came across the dark brown herd. Men were dressed in white rabbit skins, a fillet of white skin round their foreheads and a strip of the same round their wrists, for reindeer love the white and are attracted to it. Hunters proceeded in pairs, the foremost carrying in one hand the horns and part of the skin of a caribou head, in the other a small bundle of twigs. From time to time, he rubbed the horns, in a way peculiar to caribou, practiced and perfected over the ten millennia Dene have hunted in this land. The rearmost snow-shoed hunter trod exactly in the footsteps of his comrade, approaching the herd by degrees, the pair raising their legs slowly, deliberately, but setting them down somewhat swiftly, after the manner of caribou, and always taking care to lift right and left foot in unison. One knelt and vibrated his crossbow from side to side imitating the horns of a deer rubbing his head against a stone.

If any of the herd left off their feeding and pawing at the snow to gaze upon this extraordinary phenomenon, the hunters froze in their tracks, the caribou head began licking a shoulder or doing other suchlike reindeer things, until without the slightest display of suspicion, the hunters attained the very center of the herd. There at their leisure they picked out the fattest, let fly their shot, and two beasts dropped. The herd scrambled off through the snow, but others cried "Hou! Hou!"–cupping their hands to make their voices carry. With the deep stupidity of herded things, the animals retraced their steps, came straight at the hunters, and the Dene decimated them, until the remnants of the herd smelt blood. Bewildered, terrorized, they fled in all directions, dashing from the lakeside into the woods, scaling rocks, some with mouths open showing a foot of black tongue. There one might see, as they ran, the slanting of arrows. At each turn in the woods, a shaft shot through the air, bit into the brown hide with its broad head. "What!" they cried out as they died in the snow, where they brayed and bled. *"Ekfwen!"* hunters yelled, *"Ekfwen!"*–Dene for flesh, the sweetest in the north.

So the Chief hunted along the edge of the woods, while that fine officer, Gavin McHenry, all curtained about, lay snug in his bed under a luxurious cover, while a late rising sun streamed against the walls. And as he slumbered, he heard the slyest, barely perceptible sound at his door that opened ever so slightly ajar. He raised his head out of the bedclothes, just a little, caught up the corner of the curtain, and warily waited a moment to see what this might be.

It was the lady, loveliest to behold. Gently, almost fastidiously, she drew the door closed behind her and made toward the bed. The young officer blushed, adroitly laid himself down, and let on that he was still asleep. Silently she tiptoed forward, stole toward his bed, brushed back the curtain, and crept within. Soft and full, she sat herself on the bedside and lingered there the longest time to see when he would waken. The lad lay there a full long while as he compassed in all his conscience what this case might mean and where it might lead–for it seemed to him quite a marvelous thing.

Yet he said to himself, "Probably it would be better to spell out exactly what she wants." He wakened, stretched, and turning towards her, opened his eyelids; then feigning surprise, he made the sign of the cross as if seeking protection from the Holy Mother herself. With the sweetest of chin and cheeks, all tawny copper red, fragrant and dark, from the smallest of laughing lips, she gracefully said, "Good morning, Gavin. You're an unwary sleeper to let someone slip in here. Now you're taken, on the spot. Unless we come to some agreement, trust me, I'll bind you right here in your bed." All laughing, the lady launched her little sortie.

"Good morning, yourself!" Gavin said, as blithely as he was able. "Do what you like with me; I can live with that. I give up and throw myself on the mercy of the court–best thing, too, in my judgment, since I seem to have little choice." So he joked in return with as much cheerful laughter as he could muster. "But, my dear, lovely lady, kindly grant me leave, release this prisoner of yours, and allow him to rise. If I could get out of this bed and put on proper clothes, I'd be ever so much more comfortable–and, yes, I might even be prepared to talk."

"Oh, no, my good man. Honestly," the charming woman said, "You're not going to budge from that bed. I'll go you one better. I'll cuff you here on the other side too, and chat on with the man I've caught, for I'm well aware who you are. You, sir, are Gavin McHenry, officer of the Royal Canadian Mounted Police, that all the world admires; wherever you go, your honour and courtesy are praised to the skies by chiefs, by ladies, by all in the north. And now you're right here, and we're all by ourselves. My husband and his men are far away. The door is closed and set with a good strong hasp. Others bide in their beds, my own servants, too. And since I have in this house the man everyone loves, I'll just as well make the most of my time while it lasts. You're welcome to my body, for your pleasure and delectation. A fine, subtle force urges me forward. 'Serve him!' it tells me, and so I will."

Young Gavin wasn't quite sure what to make of this remarkable declaration, so he decided to pretend it had never occurred.

"In all good faith," he said, "I think I'm ahead quite enough already, though I'm actually not the man you speak of. To reach such heights of reverence the way you've just rehearsed them for me—well, I'm totally unworthy; I know very well myself. But, oh my god, I *would* be glad—mind you, only if you thought it a good thing—if by some word or deed I could be of service to you, support you, raise up your reputation—now that for me would be a real joy."

The lady gaily replied, "In the very same 'good faith', Officer McHenry, this stature of yours and—dare I say prowess others find so pleasing, if I disparaged or made light of it in any way, now *that* would hardly be nice of me, would it? I mean there are plenty of ladies who'd much rather have you in their clutches, my dear young man, as I have here, to dally and talk with, to furnish them some comfort and smooth away cares than all the gold or other fancy treasure they might already possess. And while I do love the Lord above who keeps the heavens from falling, by His grace, I might add, I have right here in my own hands what everyone in the world desires." So she brought him good cheer, she of so fair a face, but to each and every case, young Gavin offered a discreet and seemly answer.

"Madame," said Gavin merrily, *en français,* "I hope Mother Mary repays you for your truly outstanding generosity. Other people may get credit for good deeds, but the hospitality you've shown me here, totally unexpected, I don't in the least deserve. You're the one who should be worshipped. You know nothing but goodness."

"By the same Mother Mary," the Chief's wife replied, smiling, "I think differently. If I were worth all the treasure of women alive and held all the wealth of the world in my very own hands, and if I could bargain and choose myself a husband, for all the values I've seen in you, Gavin

McHenry–handsome, yes, debonair, charming–everything I've heard and now know to be true–no man on earth could be chosen before you."

"Oh dear, I swear to god, you're worth more than anyone," the young man declared, "and you've fared a whole lot better. Still, I'm proud of your high opinion of me, and I'll tell you something in all seriousness. I would like to look on you the same way an officer of the crown would look on the sovereign he's sworn to serve."

So they chitchatted of this and that till well past mid-morning, and all the while the lady let on that she was very much in love with him. Yet Gavin mounted a deft and gracious defense. Though she was the loveliest woman he could ever conceive, love weighed on him less than the object he sought–the smash with a sword that he had to endure, that dire thing that needed to be done. When the lady spoke of leaving, he was quick to agree.

She bade him good-bye and then with a glance, laughed, and astounded him with this rebuke: "God lets each speech prosper, I know. And may He repay you the pleasure. But there's no way you could possibly be Gavin McHenry."

"Why not?" demanded the young constable, quick with his question, fearing he'd failed in some aspect of proper procedure.

"Oh, bless you!" she replied. "Here's why. So specially good as Gavin McHenry is known to be, so gentlemanly and closed up in himself, ever so clean and pure, he could never have spent so much time with a lady without craving a little courteous kiss, at the end of some silly remark, or at some tiny touch or trifle."

Then Gavin said, "Well, if you find it worthwhile, I'll kiss on command, as befits an officer of the crown, and so as not to displease you, I'll do whatever you ask of me. No need to insist."

With that, she came near, caught him in her arms, leaned gracefully over, and kissed the lad on both cheeks, as the French do, and since this was the Christmas season, they commended each other to Christ's keeping. She went toward the door without further ado, and he stretched to rise, jumped out of bed, called to the chambermaid, chose his clothes, and when he was ready, made his way blithely to mass. Then he went to a dinner all splendidly laid out for him and had a grand time playing games and amusing himself all day long until moonlight. Never did a lad so suitably sit between two such distinguished ladies, the old and the young. Such joy they had together!

CHAPTER 9

And still the fine Chief of those aboriginal lands was bent on his sport, hunting wood caribou by the frozen lakeside. Such a slew of bulls and cows he'd slaughtered by sundown, I deem it a wonder. Then finally folk came flocking in, skidded the caribou to shore, quickly made a snow quarry for the slain beasts, and kindled a fire. The ablest pressed forward with assistants enough, gathered together the fattest there were, searched them at assay, and fittingly dismembered them as the task demanded. Two fingers of fat they found on the worst.

They slit the base of the throat, seized the second stomach, scraped it with a keen knife, and knit it up. Then a cut was made around the neck and via the antlers the head twisted to break it from the body. Next starting at the neck, natives ran their knives under the hide, right down to the tail, took care not to penetrate the belly, then cut the hide out to each hoof at the inside of the leg. They ripped the skin back from each limb, pulled it off the carcass from top to bottom, and lay it open on the snow to freeze, hair side down. Then they broke open the belly and took out the bowels. Heart, liver, kidneys, and stomach were put to one side, along with the fetus, where one existed, a true Dene delicacy, together with warble fly larvae, spooned up from parasite nests in the not yet frozen hides and collected in bottles for kids who found them better than jellybeans.

Then men grasped the throat, skillfully parted gullet from windpipe, and tossed the guts. Sharp knives shore through the shoulder bones, that men slid through a small hole to maintain the sides whole. To keep them from freezing, hunters buried their knives in the hindquarters and picked up their axes to chop open the breast and split it in two. And once more men worked at the throat, roundly rived it right to the leg fork, cleaned off the innards, and as if with a surgeon's scalpel, rapidly they lanceted out the rib-fillets. So, as is correct, they rid themselves of the offal near the spine, right down to the haunches that hung from it in one piece. There where the hind legs forked, they sliced the folds behind, hurrying to hack the beast in two and unbind its backbone. Both the head and the neck they hewed off next, quickly sundered the side from the chine, then skewered each thick slab through the ribs, hanging them by the hocks of their legs and tossing them onto the sleigh. Each beast took no more than seven minutes to butcher so. According to custom, on a fine moose hide, they fed their dogs, with liver and lungs and the linings of stomachs and bannock bathed in blood, all blended together. Ribs were quickly roasted over the roaring fire, and some Dene hunters could not wait, but must singe the hair off the lower leg and eat the Achilles tendon raw, so delicious did they find it.

Then, on their return, the Chief commanded everyone to gather in the lodge and summoned the ladies and the chambermaids, in front of all of which fine folk he ordered his caribou meat fetched and piled up on the floor, and with the playfullest of good grace, he called Gavin over, totted up his tally of plump beasts, and showed him the splendid slices shorn from the ribs.

"How paying is this kind of play, eh? Have I won some praise here? Haven't I served my craft and earned your thanks for thriving this well?"

"Yes indeed," replied Gavin. "The finest winter caribou I've seen in seven years, I swear."

"And I give it to you, Gavin," the man declared. "I give it all to you, for by the terms of our covenant you may claim it as your own."

"Just so," the young man said. "And I might say the same to you. What I've been worthy enough to win here within these walls, I give to you with all the good will you plainly deserve."

And he hasped the Chief's fair neck in his arms and kissed him on both cheeks in as comely a fashion as he could devise. "My catch of the day, sir. Take it. I got nothing more. I yield it up freely, and would even if it were finer."

"This is very good!" mused the grand Chief. "Thank you for that. But it might be so much the better if you'd tell me where, by your own devices, you won such a thing."

"No such clause in our contract, so you can't really ask more. Now you've taken what you're owed, in all fairness you can expect nothing further."

They laughed and joked together, then went to supper to dine on more dainties and delicacies, all entirely fresh and new.

And soon thereafter they sat by the fire in the Chief's chambers, well-wishers bringing them their choice of whiskeys, and once again they jokingly agreed to fulfill the exact pledge they'd made before: whatever occurred, at night when they met, they'd exchange their winnings, whichever new things that were fit to be named. So before the whole hall, they struck the same deal. Strong drink was fetched in the best of spirits, and the Chief told Gavin of the grizzly that had stalked the caribou killing field the day before.

"Most did not see him, but I saw him," the Chief said. "He has no fear of man."

"How do you know?"

"Because he was too hungry for wintertime. I yelled at him, and he went back into the woods, but as we cut the caribou, he kept coming back. He is an unhappy bear. Dangerous."

Then graciously at last they took their leave; each man bustled off to bed, and by the time the cock had crowed and cackled a mere three times, the Chief had leapt out of bed along with his men, did breakfast and mass, and before day had sprung, they'd dressed their ranks and made for the woods to chase bear. Through drifting snow, they passed as if through space, the Eskimo dogs uncoupled, barking, bounding amongst thick stands of aspen, some still clinging to their yellowed leaves. By the lakeside, a few caught their quarry's scent, and with wild words and noises the Chief urged on those who'd found it first. The dogs that heard him raced in haste through the snow, fell in together on the scent trail, a dozen at once. There rose such a glaver and din of men and Eskimo dogs the rocks about rang out. With yells and shouts, natives hardened canine hearts, as the mad assembly made its way between a spiked crag and a steaming pool, strangely unfrozen in that aspen stand. On a knoll by the poolside cliff, there where half covered with snow, rough rocks had fallen and strewn themselves pell-mell, dogs picked their way toward their prey, their masters right behind them.

They staked themselves round both crag and knoll, until they were sure that encircled within, was the beast the dogs had discovered. Hunters beat the bushes, baited him to rise up and come forth; then sideways, bowling over men, out bolted the most astounding bear, roaring, grim, massive, broad-shouldered, the greatest of all imaginable grizzly boars, terrible to behold. He stood to his twelve-foot height, at one blow swatted three Eskimo dogs to the ground, and then sped away, scot-free, no further damage done. Others hallooed after him, at the top of their lungs shouting "Hi!" and "Hay! Hay!" Noisily, they hurried after this beast to corner him, hunters and Eskimo dogs alike, all primed for the kill. Often that grizzly bear stood at bay and maimed members of the pack. Badly hurt, they yowled and yelped piteously.

Men pressed forward to shoot at him, loosed arrows, but hit him only occasionally, so wary were they of that giant beast, and those that struck could not pierce his bristling fur, thick as a coat of armour, except for one that frenzied him with such brain-mad rage he rushed at the men, injuring so many that like the dogs, they became afraid and drew back from the fray. Not so the Chief, who carried on after that savage grizzly boar until the sun began to set. With such deeds that day they drove themselves on, while our lovely lad lay in his bed, Gavin McHenry, happily at home, in his gorgeous clothes of many colours. Nor did the lady neglect to come and salute him; early enough was she at him, to get him to change his mood.

She came to the curtain and peeped in at the young man. Gavin at once politely welcomed her, and replying in kind, she sat herself softly by his side, suddenly laughed, and with a charming look, laid down these words: "Sir, if you are really Gavin McHenry – and I'm starting to wonder – how could a person so completely wedded to goodness not understand the rules of decent company? And when someone makes you aware of them, you cast them utterly aside and out of mind! Have you forgotten what I taught you yesterday, in the truest words I could muster?"

"What's that?" asked Gavin. "I have no idea. If what you're saying is accurate, the blame's all mine."

"But I taught you about *kissing*, silly. And how to claim favours back quickly when one is given. That is how courteous officers of the crown conduct themselves."

"My dear lady, please don't say such things," the young man murmured half under his breath. "I didn't dare do that in case I'd be refused. If you spurned such advances, I'd be wrong to have made them."

"Ma foi, monsieur!" cried the merry wife. "Who could refuse you? Besides, you're stiff and strong, sir, enough to *constrain* with strength, if you liked – if any were so ill-bred as to resist you."

"Perhaps, ma'am," Gavin declared, "you do indeed say some good things, but where I come from, threats like that aren't well received and neither are gifts not given with good will. I'm at your command, to give kisses when you like. You may take one at your pleasure, and leave off when you choose."

She bent down over him and in the comeliest way, kissed his cheek. Then much talk they devoted to love's trials and toil, its grief and its grace, for the lady plainly said, "I'd like to learn from you, sir, if it's not too bothersome, what skills you might possess, so young and fit as you are, so courteous and, may I say, knightly—like Mr. Knightly himself! You see how I've read my novels and can hardly conceal my insatiable curiosities. The thing women hold in highest regard is the practice of love. There is the literature of arms, and its chief handmaiden is love. Men stake their lives on her, suffer her pangs, through valour, wreak vengeance on the miseries she inflicts, and so bring ineffable bliss to her bowers and bedrooms with bounties utterly her own. That is the title and the text of a true man's works, as it's been through the ebb and flow of myths and tales from the dawn of time. Yet here you are, an outstanding young man of your day; your fame and your honour walk alongside every trail in the north, and I have sat by you here on two separate occasions yet have never heard from out of your head a single word that could be said to belong to love, neither less nor more. And you, sir, ever so courteous and mannerly in your vows and commitments, ought to be yearning to show a young thing like me and teach her some token of the intricate craft of love. You've almost made me lose patience with you! What! Are you ignorant, my silly Mr. Famous-One? Or am *I* deemed too daft to hearken to your dalliances? For shame! I'm almost *cross* with you, and I won't endure it! I come here, single and alone, and sit to learn and be enlightened about love. I *could* say crass things like 'Put some lead in your pencil,' but I won't. However, I do want you to show me some of your expertise while my husband is far from home."

"May God reward you," said Gavin, "In good faith. It gives me great joy and is a huge privilege that someone as gifted as you should find your way here to my room and trouble yourself with so poor a fellow, play with a simple constable, and flatter him with your favours. But for me to take on the task of explaining true love, to touch on the topic of feats of arms with you, who I'm well aware, have more sleight of mind by half than a hundred like me ever could, no matter how long I live, well now, that would be the height of folly, my dear lady, I swear it. I'd do your bidding to the best of my abilities, because I'm greatly beholden to you, and will always be your loyal servant, so help me God."

So that woman continually tried and tempted him, whatever else she thought, to win him over to caprice and wickedness, but he so fairly defended himself that no fault appeared on either side, and if evil be forever explicit, they knew nothing but bliss. They laughed and lingered, and then at last she kissed him, charmingly took her leave, and went her way.

CHAPTER 10

Gavin roused himself to get ready for mass, for it was the Christmas season again, only one year later. Afterwards dinner was prepared and formally served. The young lad and his ladies dallied all day, but the Chief snow-shoed through the woods, after that menacing grizzly boar that plowed by the riverbanks and then when he stood at bay, mauled the backs of the Eskimo dogs with his fierce paws. Finally, bowmen broke his cover and forced him into the open, so fast the arrows flew where folk had gathered. But the stoutest-hearted he startled and they edged back until at last, he was so tired he could run no more, but with what speed he had left, made his way to a hole near a boulder at the burnside. He got the bank of the stream at his back, rose on his haunches to his full height, bit the air, and froth foamed at his mouth like a foul mess, drooled down his lips, black against the white fangs.

An irksome time it was for the brave men who stood round trying to wound him from afar, because their crossbows were slow and none dared come closer for fear of injury. He'd hurt so many already, all were loath to be torn by those claws, so brain-mad and frenzied a bear he was. Until the Chief himself came, encouraging his dogs, saw that grizzly boar standing at bay, ringed by his men, and leaving his dogs behind, nimbly approached despite the snow. Carrying a seven-foot spear, he strode forth big time, hastened quickly by the stream toward the waiting bear. The wild thing saw him with his weapon in hand and roared so fiercely many feared the Chief would get the worst of it. The animal charged out, straight at his tormentor, so that hunter and beast lay both in a heap amid the deep snow. The other had the worse. For the man

kept him well in his sights as they first met and thrust the spear firmly into the pit of his chest, drove it right through his body, shattering his heart. With a hideous snarl, then a ghostly moan, the bear yielded up his spirit in the bloodied snow. A half dozen Eskimo dogs seized him, bravely bit into his body, and as men dragged him from the snow bank, the dogs finished him off.

A man who was wise in the ways of woodcraft began skillfully butchering this bear. He slit the skin right to the paws and peeled it from the body like a sock, rolled up the hide with the head intact, and placed it in a bag on the sled. Then from the strangely human carcass he removed the fats, both tallow and gluten, lest they render the meat rancid, cut the beast in broad, glistening slabs, fastened halves together, all whole, and afterwards laid them out on the sleigh. Both dogs and men headed eagerly for home. Staring gruesomely from the top of the sack, bobbing to and fro, the bear's head was carried before the rest of the hunters by the Chief himself, who'd killed it near a frozen stream by force of his own strong hand.

Till he set eyes on Gavin, the Chief found things in the lodge rather dull. But he called for him, and the young man gladly came forward to claim his reward. The Chief could be loud at times, in his speech and his hearty laughter, and when he saw Gavin he spoke with great comfort and joy. The good ladies were fetched and the gang all gathered, then he showed off the slabs of meat and told them the tale of how long, how large, and how very lethal this bear had been and of the battle with the wild beast in the woods where he'd fled. Graciously, Gavin commended his prowess and lauded him for the fortitude he clearly possessed, for never, the young officer said, had there ever been seen so brawny a bruin or such fine sides of meat. Hunters patted and handled that huge head, still attached to its skin, pricked their fingers against fangs that had bitten the backs of so many dogs, and so the Chief could hear, the adroit young man both praised and recoiled from it in horror, only partially feigned.

"Now, Gavin," said his host, "as you well know, this prize is yours, by contract, fair and square."

"So it is," the young man agreed, "and just as true, as pledged, all my gains I return to you."

He clasped the Chief about the neck, kissed him handsomely on one cheek, and then straightway served him again on the other in the same style.

"Now we're even this evening," the young man declared, "in all clauses of the contract agreed since I came."

"St. Giles protects cripples," the Chief laughed, "but not this bear. You, my boy, are the best! You'll be rich in a bit, if you keep driving bargains like this."

Then long tables were set up with benches to match, lights turned on, table cloths spread out, as chambermaids laid out settings and served all who sat down. There was glee; there was glam galore, Dene style, before a huge fire in the slate fireplace, and during supper and afterwards, native chants, songs, Christmas carols, dances, as much mirth and merriment as man could devise. And all the while sat Gavin McHenry, careful and always courteous, beside the Chief's wife. Such a semblance of love for the young man did she make with stolen, furtive glances meant to please and encourage, that he became utterly flummoxed, even vexed with himself, but placing nurture above nature, he would not spurn her, but dealt with her behaviour in the daintiest way he could manage, however his motives might be construed. When playtime in that great hall had lasted as long as the Grand Chief liked, he called Gavin to his room for a fireside chat.

And there they dealt with one another, drank, and the Chief determined to renew the same arrangement for New Year's Eve. Gavin begged leave to depart that morning for it was near time he should go, but the Chief wouldn't let him, prolonged his stay, and said, "I'll speak honestly. Word of honour, my friend, you'll reach the Green Chapel and do your chores by dawn New Year's, well before nine. So lie in your bed and take your ease, and I'll go hunting in the snow, for my men spotted a coyote they don't like and want his pelt to decorate their benches."

"Why don't they like him?"

The Chief grew pensive, paused a while, then looked toward his companion.

"Because one day our people thought we were too many here in the Nahanni Valley and some should die, be gone for a while, and then return. It was Coyote who jumped up and said people should die forever, since there wasn't enough food to feed everybody. Others said, 'How could there be happiness in the world if our loved ones die and are gone forever? People will grieve and become anxious.' So our medicine men found a cave near the river, and there they sang songs that called the spirits of the dead to come forth so they could be restored to their former selves and live with us again.

"A wind sprang up, and a handsome warrior beheaded by our enemies appeared and was restored. Everyone was happy, except Coyote. He was mad his rules had not been respected. So he sat at the entrance to the cave, and when he heard the wind again around him, he rolled some rocks in front of the cave, and the wind whirled on by. Now when we hear the wind whistling, we say someone is wandering the earth trying to get home. Coyote, he leapt up and ran away, because he was afraid for what he had done. Now he scurries from one place to the next, always looking over his shoulder to see who is after him. We never feed him. We hunt him, kill him, and use his skin to warm ourselves in the cold."

Then the Chief grew hearty again, smiled, and said to Gavin, "So I'm going hunting in the woods, and you, my friend, must keep to the contract, exchange winnings with me when I come back, because I've tested you twice and found you a faithful sort of fellow. But tomorrow morning, remember! *Third time throw best.* Now let's have a good time while we can and think only of joy and pleasure, since we can have misery whenever we like."

"I'll grant you that!" Gavin laughed, and he stayed.

Drinks came; then they both went to bed. Gavin lay and slept all soft and still the whole night through, but the Chief kept to his hunting in the late dawn light. He grabbed a bite to eat, his dogs and men at the ready. A pale red sun, ragged with cold, drove racks from the firmament, clearing the sky of every cloud, and the Nahanni uplands sparkled with frost. Hunters freed the dogs from their traces, and some picked up Coyote's scent there where he hid; then he cross-tracked or by dint of his foxy wiles, trailed off on a tangent. A smaller Eskimo dog barked, and his fellows fell in with him, panting from thick-fogged lungs, as they ran forth in a rabble, right on his tail. Coyote frisked lightly ahead in the snow, but they soon found his trail, and when they caught sight of him, quickly gave chase, cursing him with a wrathful din. He twisted and turned through dense aspen stands, and then doubled back, listening by the side of bushes not yet drowned in snow. At last he jumped over a sulfur spring and crept stealthily by the edge of an ice-free pond, thinking with his wily ways he was half out of the woods and beyond the dogs. But before he knew it, all at once, he found himself ambushed by three of the largest. He blenched in fear, then dismayed and woebegone, speedily sprang away again to the bush.

But winter's joy it was to hear the dogs bay, when the pack, all roused and mingled together, came upon Coyote, and the cry they set on his head at that sight was as if all the clustering cliffs of the Nahanni National Park had come clattering down in heaps. Here he was yelled at, when hunters happened upon him, snarled at with loud jeers. There he was threatened, often called thief, no time to tarry, always with dogs on his tail. When out in the open, he was almost run down. Often he doubled back, so wily was Reynard Coyote. And yes! The last of those men would lag far behind, led astray in this way till mid-afternoon fell in the wild Mackenzie Mountains, while warm at home our able officer of the crown wholesomely slept, behind comely bed curtains, there on a cold morning.

Was it love that let the lady neither sleep nor impair the purpose pitched in her heart? She got herself up straightaway, and in a charming dress, brushing the ground, one trimmed with the finest fur, the purest of pelts, she rushed to his room. No scarf graced her head, but heavenly gemstones in clusters of twenty studded her hair. Her lovely face and throat were thrown open, all naked, her breast bare before, her back as well. She came in at the bedroom door and closed it after her, swooshed up a window, and called out to Gavin, cheerfully rebuking him with these choice words: "Hey, man! How can you sleep on so clear a morning?"

He was drowsing deeply, yet he could hear her.

CHAPTER 11

Gavin McHenry was muttering in his sleep, as if from the depths of dreams, darkest at dawn, those of a man caught in the throes of thought about how the next day, at a Green Chapel, destiny would deal him his fate, there where he must meet a monstrous giant of a man, a Sasquatch, elegant for all that, and without further debate abide a deadly blow from a curved Turkish sword. But when that comely beauty appeared, he recovered his wits, swung out of his dreams, and hastily replied. The lovely lady came laughing, sweet, and he felt her hair fall over his fair face as she politely kissed his cheek, and he welcomed her cheerily in the best of taste. He saw her so glorious and gaily attired, so faultless in her features and of so fine a dark cedar hue, a flush of rapture warmed his heart. All was bliss and bonhomie between them, smitten as they were by smiles and by mirth. Fine words flowed, with much good cheer therein, but alas, great peril stood between them, too, had Mother Mary not minded her charge.

For that Dene princess pressed him so thickly, pushed him so near the brink, he felt obliged either to take her love on the spot or like a boor, refuse it. He cared about simple courtesy, about uncouth things, even more about mischief and the makings of sin, about treating the Chief of that lodge, as would the basest of traitors.

"God forbid!" the young man said. "That for sure won't happen."

With affectionate laughter he laid aside all the speeches of *spécialité*, whatever the source, all the blandishments that sprang from her mouth. Then the woman said to him, "You'll deserve nothing but blame if you don't love the living creature lying next to you, before all women alive wounded in her heart – unless you already have a girlfriend, a lover you like better, and have promised yourself to her, fastened yourself so hard you can't break the bond – which is what I now believe. Tell me truly. I'm asking you. For all the love in the world, don't hide the truth with guile." Why those lines from the old movie he'd watched that past summer suddenly occurred to him, Gavin McHenry couldn't say. "God has a big heart. But there is one sin he will not forgive. If a woman calls a man to her bed, and he will not go."

And there were other sins to contend with, besides. Nelson Poundmaker came to mind, and he found himself telling her about his girlfriend, the baby he'd made her get rid of, that living thing torn from her womb, hunted and butchered like caribou, his own flesh and blood, eyes slit closed as he imagined them to be, its sweet head unfinished, not fully grown, and he felt a powerful remorse while he confessed his part in this. All at once it hit home to him that his progeny, the children of his lineage, his own paternity would never learn of his ordeal, never ponder what it might mean, or spend a moment at his grave to mourn and remember him.

"Zorba! Teach me to dance!"

But these, he knew, were not the dances Nelson Poundmaker had had in mind.

"That is the worst of all," said the lady, "but you've given me my answer, really, and a painful one, too. Kiss me, and I'll be on my way and spend my time grieving, as may those who love too fondly."

Sighing, she bent down and politely kissed him, then severing from him, glanced at his keychain, with its moon and five pointed star, the Latin words beneath, *Solus virtus nobilitat*. Then she said as she stood, "Now, my dear, do me in parting this favour; give me something as your gift, this keychain perhaps, so I might think of you and lessen my sadness."

He could see she was curious, but he did not translate the words. Instead he said simply, "I know for your sake I'd prefer to have the handsomest thing in the world, for you've really deserved – and I don't know how often – more by rights than I could ever repay. But to give you some worthless thing as a keepsake, let alone a keychain, does you no honour. I'm here on an errand in a wild land. I have no men with bagsful of expensive things, and I don't much like that, my lady, for your sake, especially now, but each man must do as he must, so don't be hurt or take offence."

"No, my most honourable sir," that lovesome one smiled. "I get naught from you, I see, but you shall have something from me."

She proffered him the richest ring worked in red gold with a glittering stone standing proudly aloft and shedding its blushing beams like the bright sun. Take note; it was worth a huge sum! But Gavin refused and said straightaway, "In God's name, I want no gifts at this time. I have nothing to offer you, so I'll take nothing in return."

She busily insisted, and he just as firmly refused, swearing swiftly on his word as an officer of the law that he would not and could not lay a hand on it. She was sorry that he'd foresworn what to her was a trifle and said thereafter, "If you say no to my ring because it seems too rich a gift and you don't want to be beholden to me, I'll give you my sash instead, and that gains you less."

Deftly she undid a gorgeous *ceinture fléchée* wrapped round her waist, fastened over her gown, and finger woven of green, red, and white strands of wool, trimmed with gold and embroidered at the edges with beads and hand-stitched ornaments. And this she offered to Gavin McHenry, and in her blithe manner, she beseeched him to take it, unworthy as it was. Again he said no, in no way would he touch either keepsake or gold, before God sent him grace enough to achieve the task he'd chosen there. "And so I beg you, don't be displeased, and let go this

business, because I'll never be able to grant it. I *am* deeply beholden to you, because you've been so kind. Whether the wind blows hot or the wind blows cold, I'll always be at your service."

"Now, are you refusing this sash," the lady then said, "Because it is so simple? So it may seem. Look, it's a small thing and worth even less. But anyone who knew the value knitted up here would perhaps appraise its properties at a higher price. For whoever girds his loins with this green sash, while he has it tied all tightly round his winter coat, there's no man under heaven who can hew him down, since by any sleights of this earth, he cannot be slain."

The young man pondered, and it came home to him, straight to his heart, this was a jewel, a talisman of a *ceinture fléchée* meant to ward off whatever jeopardy awaited him: a splendid stratagem to slip out unslain after gaining the Green Chapel to be given his final checkmate.

He put up with her pleading and let her speak, and she in turn put pressure to bear that he take this woolen belt that she offered once more. Then he relented, gave in with good grace–and she implored him, for her sake, never to reveal it, but loyally hide it from her husband. Gavin indeed agreed, no matter what, that never a soul but they two should know of their secret. Time and again he thanked her, in his head and in his heart, by which time she'd thrice kissed her valiant officer of the crown.

Then she prepared to go and left him there, for more satisfaction from that young man she was not about to receive. When she'd gone, Gavin quickly got himself ready, rose, dressed himself in splendid native array, and laid aside the love token the lady had provided, hid it carefully where he could find it later. Promptly he then chose his way to a chapel, privily approached a priest, and prayed that he might raise his spirit upward, the better to instruct him how his soul might be saved when he saw heaven. Then he fairly shrove himself, revealing all his misdeeds, both the greater and the lesser, and begging forgiveness, humbly called on the priest for absolution. And he absolved him with certainty and set him so clean Doomsday could have been declared the day after. And then Gavin made merry with the fine ladies, with charming songs and gaiety of all kinds, as never he did before that day, far into the blissful night. Each man he treated with the utmost deference, and they all declared since he'd come, they'd never seen him quite so merry.

Long may he linger, and love come his way! The Chief was still in the bush, leading his men. He'd finished off this coyote he'd followed for so long. As he clambered over a rock to look for the rascal, he heard the Eskimo dogs harrying him. Coyote, he who'd made death permanent, came bounding through a snow-covered thicket, six dogs howling on his heels. The Chief caught sight of that wild thing, and warily watching, cocked his crossbow and let fly at the beast. Coyote shied away from the arrow and tried to turn back, but a dog rushed at him, just before he could, and almost on top of the man's snowshoes, they all fell on him and worried away at the wily one with a wrathful din.

The Chief straightaway grabbed Coyote's body, snatched it out of the dogs' mouths, held it on high over his head, and loudly hallooed, while a dozen Eskimo dogs stood snarling about. Native hunters hurried towards him, and when that fine band was all assembled, they raised a giant shout in the snowy woods, the richest clamour, as dinful a hymn for Coyote's soul as ever men heard. Hunters rewarded their dogs, rubbed and patted their heads, and then they took thieving Coyote and stripped him of his coat.

And then they headed for home, for it was nearly nightfall. At last in front of his well-loved lodge, the Chief alighted from his sled, found a roaring fire in the hearth, beside it that good young man, Gavin McHenry, officer of the crown, completely content and taking great pleasure in the company of the ladies. He wore the same magnificent

Pendleton coat of many colours, fur-lined with lynx and rabbit, maroon in hue but interspersed with oranges, greens, and cobalt blues in long trailing lines of patterns and shapes, like the Muslim geometry of God, all order, balance, and intricate juxtaposition.

He met the grand Chief in the middle of the floor, playfully greeted him, and said fittingly, "First I'll fulfill the terms of our contract, the one we readily agreed to when there was plenty to drink." Then he embraced the Chief and kissed him three times, as steadily and soberly as he thought correct.

"Jesus Christ," said the Chief, "You'll do yourself proud with these sorts of profits, if the price was right."

"Never mind about the price," Gavin quickly rejoined, "since I've properly paid for the purchase I made."

"Well," said the other, "Mine's the loser, then, for I've hunted all day long and got nothing but this miserable coyote skin, devil take it–poor payment for the precious things you've pressed on *me*, three such kisses, each one so good."

"Enough," declared Gavin. "Thank you. Case closed." And as they stood there, he heard about how Coyote was killed.

With mirth and music and meats of all sorts, they made as merry as might any men that night, with ladies' laughter and jokes everywhere. Gavin and the Grand Chief were both so glad it was as if the whole group had gone either mad or drunk. The Chief and his men played many pranks until the time came when they had to part and folks at last had to take to their beds. Then humbly Gavin McHenry took his leave from the Chief and thanked him profusely: "For such a wonderful sojourn as I've had here, honoured by you at this great feast, may God reward you. I'd offer to be one of your own tribe, if you liked, but as you know, tomorrow morning I need to move on. And if as you promised, you could give me some guide to show me the way to the green chapel, then God will allow me to suffer the fate I have in store on New Year's Day."

"Honestly," said the Chief, "I'll make ready everything I ever promised you, and with the best will in the world."

Then he assigned a servant to set Gavin on his way and guide him from the suntrap lodge without delay, so he could sled through the bush by the shortest trail. Gavin again thanked the Chief for his uncommon courtesies, and then from the amiable ladies took his leave.

With regrets and with kisses he spoke to them both, earnestly thanked them, and they replied in kind, commending him to Christ with sorrowful sighs. Then with the utmost grace he bid good-bye to that household, and to each Dene tribesman he met, he offered a special thank you for the solicitous service and the pains they'd all taken, busying themselves so thoroughly for his welfare. And each man was as sorry to see him go as if they'd lived with that young officer forever. Then chambermaids led him to his room, and he was cheerfully brought to his bed and rest.

Whether or not he slept soundly is a matter of some conjecture, for that evening after holiday merriment, he had much on his mind to ponder should he so choose–of love and its final moments, of sin and the cleansing of sin, of beauty and terror. For young Gavin McHenry clung to his life and all it contained: spring's rushing streams, snow-deep woods, silent, boreal, and thick, summer's crazed northern sun. Fiercely he loved them, and that precious, secret thing, tucked beneath his pillow, his *ceinture fléchée*, the saving lie from which he'd been inexplicably absolved, *that* he could never foreswear, though he both treasured and loathed it, and though it caused him deeper pain than he'd ever before felt in his brief life. In all his conscience, he could not compass this case. There rose prominently before him the five points of Solomon's Holy Truth, the key-chain totem he'd refused to give away.

"Stories are not worth sons," he heard Nelson Poundmaker say. Poor Gavin. He could not grasp the meaning of that witch's thing tucked carefully beneath his pillow, Eve's special fruit, changeable as the day. Did it make his bed green, the beams of his house cedar, its rafters fir? Let him lie there still, since he's close to what he sought. And if you'll be quiet just a while, I'll tell you how things turned out.

PART IV

CHAPTER 12

Now the New Year drew near, and the night passed. Daylight drove out the dark as the Deity ordained. But wild was the weather the world awoke to. Clouds cast down their cold on the earth, with well nigh enough of the north to grieve the ill clad. Bitterly snow whipped up, stinging all the forest creatures. Wind whirled in gusts, wailed off the heights, and drove deep drifts to the brink of the lodge. As he lay in his bed, Gavin listened with dread. Though his eyelids were closed, he slept very little. With each cock that crew, he knew the time had come.

He rose quickly before the day dawned, to a small bedside light glimmering in the room. Rubbing his hands one final time over its fur and fine stuff, he folded his Pendleton coat and carefully draped it on top of a chair. Then he donned his clothes to ward off the cold, the ones Nelson Poundmaker had given, his Dene winter garment with its painted circles and bars, Mukluks and mittens to match, parka edged with ermine, beaded and quilled with preening eaglets and beaver kit tails tied by true-love-knots. Nor did he forget his *ceinture fléchée*, that métisse thing with its mixture of green and red and white strands, all finger woven and edged with gold–for his own good, Gavin did not forget that. After checking his crossbow, he wrapped the sash twice round his loins with delight, that sash of green wool whose colours went well against the circles and bars of his warm winter coat. But Gavin McHenry wore his *ceinture fléchée*, sacred to all Métis, not for its great worth, nor for pride in its pendants, though polished they were, nor for the glittering gold that gleamed on its edges, but to save himself when he was obliged to submit, naked and unarmed, to suffer death with neither knife nor bow to resist. By the time that bold young man had made his way outside, he'd thanked all the Dene tribesmen who'd gathered to wish him well.

Then Peowish was ready, that tongueless sled dog, securely kenneled along with the rest, in such fine condition they were eager to pull. Gavin walked up to the dogs, examined their coats, and muttered softly to himself, swearing on his word: "Here's a tribe in this lodge with real neighbourly conduct. I wish the best to their Chief and love and happiness to his lovely wife. Out of Christian charity he's cherished a guest, kindly and honourably. God reward him and them all, every one. And if I could live any longer anywhere on this earth, I'd work to repay them, if I could."

Snowshoes across his shoulders, he led his team away from the suntrap toward the deep embankments close by, stopped for a moment to tie on his gear, and said, "Jesus Christ protect this place. May all things here go well."

Then Gavin prepared to break trail, together with the one man who'd show him the way to that grievous place where he'd receive his fateful blow. They struggled up bluffs where boughs were bare, climbed by cliffs where the cold clung. Clouds were on high, but ugly beneath, sulfur streams shrouded in mist that jeweled itself on twigs of trees in growing skeins of ice, like fairy things, white ghostly creations. Each hill had a hat, a huge cloak of mist. Brooks burst forth boiling from mountain heights, shattering white against the snow as they raced sharply down. And high in the dark morning sky, moonlit in small cloudless patches, lay the ominous green and violet and pink of Aurora Borealis. Wild was the way they took through those woods, till the late winter sun finally rose. They were near the mountain peaks, struggling through drifts of snow when the Dene guide beside him came to a sudden stop.

"Sir, I've taken you here at this time, and now you're not far from that notorious place you've spied out and inquired after so specially. But I'll tell you the truth since I care for you and you're one of those I dearly love. Better follow my advice. The place you're headed for is perilous. For in those wastes lives a man, the world's worst, for he's stern and fierce and seeks to injure, and he's larger than any man in the north, his body bigger than our best four, with feet the size of a grizzly bear's, a throwback to times long ago when the lost tribes roamed these parts and beheaded their enemies in the name of their gods. Nuk-luk, we call him. Sometimes Sasquatch, the word others use. He makes sure at the green chapel that no one, however valiant or strong, passes that place who's not battered to death by dint of his hand. He's a ruthless man, and knows no mercy, for whether trapper or prospector passes that chapel, priest or chief or any one else, for him it's as joyous to kill as to live his own life. So I'm telling you, just as truly as you stand in this snow, go there, and you'll be murdered. I'm warning you. Believe me, for sure, even if you had twenty lives to throw away. He's dwelt there forever and brought misery untold. You cannot defend yourself against his brutal blows.

"So, Gavin McHenry, let the man alone. And for your own sake get away by some other trail. Trek into different country with god's speed, and I'll get myself home again, and I'm telling you, I'll swear by the Lord and all the saints in heaven—so help me!—by the Great Manitou and every medicine man from here to Yellowknife, I'll keep your secret and never breathe a word that you ran away from this monster I know."

Merci bien," Gavin declared and then grudgingly added, "It speaks well of you, my dear man, that you wish only good for me, and that you'd keep my secret like a good fellow I do believe. But however close you kept it, if I steered clear of this place, turned and fled out of fear in the way you suggest, I'd be a cowardly officer of the crown and could never be excused. I will go to this chapel, come what may, and talk with that man about whatever subject I choose, as the fates will have it. Stern foe to deal with he may well be, equipped with his sword, but God knows how to care for his faithful servants."

"Jesus and Mary!" said the other man. "Now you've just as much spelled out that you'd willfully cause yourself harm and by your own choice lose your life. I won't stand in your way. Put your parka on your head and get your crossbow ready. You'll need it. Then sled down the clearing by the rock over there till you're brought to the bottom of this valley. Look to the left, and a little off in the bush you'll see a dale with that self-same chapel and the burly beast of a man who keeps it. Now in God's name, fare well, my valiant Gavin McHenry. For all the gold underground in the north, I wouldn't go with you or keep you company in these forests one foot further."

With that his bush guide tugged at the traces, yelled "Mush!" as loud as he could, and his sled fairly leapt over the snow trails as he left Gavin there alone.

"Good lord," swore Gavin. "I can't start moping and groaning now. God's will be done. I'm in His hands."

He signaled Peowish to pick up the pace, shoved himself through two rocks by a snow bank, and sledded down the rugged hillside right to the valley below, and then looked round him. Another suntrap! But this one savage and wild, no sign of a dwelling anywhere about, but banks on both sides, beetling and steep, and rough knuckled crags and jagged rocks that seemed to graze the clouds. Then he halted, held back the dogs, and turned his head from side to side to look for the chapel. He saw no such thing in either direction. Strange, he thought, save, not far off, a mound perhaps, a rounded barrow beside a hot spring that emerged above, cascading in torrents below, seething and frothing as if feverishly boiling. Urging his team, the officer pressed on to the mound, then attached the traces to a tree, hooking them round a rough branch. Then he went to the mound and walked around it, debating with himself what it could be. It had a hole at the end and on either side; it was all overgrown with clods of grass and all hollow within – nothing but an old cave or the crevice of an ancient crag. He couldn't make sense of it.

"Oh my God," Gavin declared, "Could this be the green chapel? Maybe Lucifer himself performs his midnight mass right here! This place is deserted, an ugly oratory, all overgrown with weeds out of season, well suited for the man clad in green to deal out his devotions as the devil wills. My sixth sense tells me now the Fiend made this bargain to destroy me here. This is the chapel of mischance. Checkmate to it! It's the damnedest little church I ever entered."

Parka on his head, crossbow slung over his shoulder, he climbed up the roof of that rough structure. At that height, from a hard rock on a bank beyond the sulfur stream, he heard a horrific noise. What! It clattered against the cliffs, as if it would cleave them in two, like one grinding a scythe on a grindstone. What! It whetted and whirred like water at a mill. What! It rushed and it rang, terrible to hear.

"My God," cried Gavin, "This stuff, I suppose, is meant in my honour, to welcome me. God's will be done. Whining won't help me here one bit. I may lose my life, but no noise is going to fill me with dread."

Then the officer called out at the top of his lungs, "Who runs this place and wants to keep an appointment with me? Gavin McHenry is waiting right here. If any man wants something, let him make his way to this spot and fast, either now or never, and state his case."

"Wait!" someone cried out from a bank above his head, "And soon enough you'll get everything I promised you."

Busily the man kept on with his din for a while, and turned back to his whetstone before he'd descend, and then he made his way by a crag and like a Dall ram, burst out of a hole fronted by a green porch, whirled out of his nook with his frightful weapon, a Turkish scimitar newly honed for dealing the blow, its massive blade arching out from the hilt—honed on a grindstone, and by its gleaming lace four feet in length, no less. And the man in green was garbed as at first, face and legs, the same, both hair and beard, except that now he strode on the ground, grandly like a moose or a bear, on the biggest of feet a man ever saw. He set the scabbard to the stones and walked beside it. When he came to the stream it had divided in three, and he hopped nimbly over some boulders and with huge strides advanced, fierce and grim, on a broad clearing patched with snow.

Gavin bowed his head slightly to this Sasquatch, but not too low, and the other said, "Now, my good fellow, I see you keep your word."

CHAPTER 13

"Gavin McHenry," said the green man, "God protect you! You're welcome indeed to my place, and you've timed your travel, as a true man should. You know the treaty agreed between us. Twelve months back you took what befell you, and agreed I should fully repay you this New Year's Day. And here we are in this valley, truly all by ourselves; here are no Dene tribesmen to separate us; we can fight, as we like. Take that parka off your head, and get your pay. Give me no more debate than I gave you then, when you whipped off my head with one go."

"No, by God," cried Gavin, "Who gave me a soul, I'll bear you no grudge for whatever harm befalls me, but keep to one stroke, and I'll stand still and offer you no resistance whatever. Do what you like."

He leant his neck a little forward, bowed, showed the snow-white flesh, and let on he had no doubts at all and would never dare show fear.

Then the man dressed in green quickly got ready, gathered up his grim sword to smite young Gavin McHenry. With all the strength in his beanstalk body, he bore it aloft and swung down fiercely as if to smash him. Had he driven it down as he'd made out, our doughty officer of the crown would have died from the blow. But Gavin glanced sideways at that curved Turkish sword as it came gliding down to earth to shatter his life, and he shrank a little with his shoulders from the sharpened steel.

Sasquatch with a flinch withheld his weapon, then rebuked the young constable with all sorts of proud words: "You're not Gavin McHenry," the monster declared, "that is oh, so good, that on hill or valley never quailed before his suspects, and now you're about to flee for fear even before you've felt any harm. I never heard of such a sissy. I never flinched or fled, my brave man, when you aimed at me, nor caviled in any way at Arthur LeMagne's. My head flew to my feet, yet I never tried to fly off. And you, before any harm's done, have all kinds of little heartaches. So call me the better man, because I deserve it."

Gavin replied, "I flinched once, and I'll do so no more. But if my head falls to these stones, it's a thing I can't restore. But hurry it up man, by whatever faith you possess, and come to the point. Deal me out my destiny, and be quick about it. I'll stand you one stroke–not starting again till your sword's hit. I give you my word."

"Let's have at you then!" cried the other, heaved it up, and looked at him as wildly as if he were mad. He swung at him savagely, not giving him a scratch, suddenly withholding his hand before any harm could be done. Gavin waited there patiently. Not a limb did he stir, but stood as still as a stone or the trunk of a tree, ratcheted down into rocky ground by a hundred roots.

Then the man in green mocked him once more: "So, now you've mended your wee heart and made it whole again, it's time to be hit. May all Arthur's praise preserve you and your precious neck, if it can."

Gavin answered, shouting in sudden rage, "Thresh on, grim reaper, with your silly scythe. You threaten far too much. I hope your heart aches in your own damned breast!"

"Well, well," that monster replied, "You speak so fiercely, right now I won't delay your little errand one minute longer."

Then he strode forward to strike, puckered his forehead in fury, his lips too. No marvel Gavin's misgivings. No hope of rescue now.

Up went the sword with its knifelike edge, and it hurtled down straight at the bare neck. And hard though he struck, he hurt him no more than to snick him on one side, so the skin was severed. Through the fair fat to the flesh fell the blade, and the shimmering blood shot to the earth over his shoulders. And when the young man saw his blood glint on the snow, he sprang with both feet more than a spear's length, snatched up his parka, crammed it on his head, cocked his crossbow, and fiercely spoke–never since he was a boy born of his mother had he ever in this world felt so buoyantly happy–"Stop your attack, sir! Give me no more. Here on this spot I've taken a stroke, no strife in return, and if you offer me more, I'll strike right back, trust me, and with full force. One stroke was due me as by contract agreed at Arthur LeMagne's. And so, man, quit it *now!*"

Sasquatch kept his distance, set his blade in the ground, leaned a little on the hilt, and looked at that young man before him in the suntrap glade; how doughty, dreadless, and devoid of fear he stood there, armed and undaunted: in his heart he loved him. Then, making fun, in a loud, booming voice and resounding tone, he said, "My brave officer of the RCMP, here in this place don't be such a Grinch! No one has slighted you or mistreated you, nor acted in any way different from the covenant sworn at Arthur LeMagne's. I promised you a stroke, and a stroke you've had. Consider yourself well paid; I release you from all ancillary rights I might possess. If I'd been nimbler, perhaps I could have smacked you a worse buffet, enough to wreak real havoc and rouse your anger.

"First I playfully threatened you with a pretend blow and caused you no rough wound at all, and I say treated you right, on account of the agreement we made on that first night, which in the spirit of truth you faithfully upheld. All your gains you gave me, as a good man should. That other feint, my friend, was for the following morning, when you kissed my lovely wife–those kisses you returned to me. For both times I delivered only two mock blows, and you came out unscathed. True men repay truly, and then feel no dread. You failed at the third, so took that blow. For it is my piece of clothing you're wearing, that *ceinture fléchée*, finger woven; I know it only too well. I know all about your kisses, your virtues too, and the wooing of my wife: I put her up to it.

"I sent her to test you, and truly I think you're one of the most stainless men that ever walked on foot. As pearls outvalue dried white peas, so, Gavin, do you outrank all your fellow officers. But here you lacked just a little, sir, and fell short in your loyalty. But that was not because of a gorgeous thing, nor for wooing either, but because you love your life, and so I blame you less."

The young man stood studying this case a long while, so stricken with guilt he was trembling within; all the blood in his breast burned in his face, and he shrank for shame at what the Chieftain had said. The first words that officer uttered were, "God damn cowardice! And Goddamn coveting other men's wives! In you lie vice and villainy that destroy a man's virtue."

Then he seized the knot, loosened it, and heaved the sash angrily toward the man.

"There it is, the foul thing, may the devil take it. Caring too much about your blow taught me cowardice, made me side with covetousness and forsake my own nature, the loyalty and liberality of a true officer. Now I'm found false and at fault, I who've always feared treachery and deceit. May sorrow and care accompany them both. I acknowledge, Chief, my reputation is ruined. Let me regain your good will. Next time I'll be more wary."

Then the other man laughed and graciously said, "No, Gavin, you may think badly about what just happened, having come face to face with your own true self, but for any harm you've done, I've been made entirely whole. You confessed so cleanly, admitted your mistakes, and at the point of my sword paid your penance, I submit you're all polished up from that sin, washed as clean as if you'd never transgressed since the day you were first born. And, sir, I give you that *ceinture fléchée*, that is hemmed in gold, for it's as green as my gown. Gavin McHenry, you may think about this meeting, there when you mingle among the high and mighty at Arthur LeMagne's, or in officers' gatherings in the RCMP, for this is the purest token of all the risks you encountered at the green chapel. And you shall come back to my lodge this cold New Year and revel full well in the remnants of that rich feast."

Then the Chief embraced him closely and said, "I venture that with my wife, who was your cunning foe, you'll come to a fine accord."

But Gavin paid little attention. Seizing his parka, he took it off in a cool rage, and then said as politely as he could, "No, I've stayed long enough already. The best of luck to you, and may He who bestows all honours richly reward you. And commend me to that courteous one, your lovely wife, both the one and the other, who with their wanton wiles so quaintly beguiled their constable. But it's no wonder if a fool acts like a madman, brought to sorrow through women's tricks. My mother warned me, as did Bishop Steinam, who knows his Bible: Adam was beguiled by one here on this earth, Solomon by many such, likewise Samson – Delilah dealt him his fate – and David thereafter, blinded by Bathsheba, suffered his own misery. Since these four were plagued by their wiles, it would be a huge win to love them well and trust them never, if a man could. These four were the best men ever known. Fortune favoured them more perfectly than anyone else on earth or in heaven, all of them beguiled by the women they dealt with. If I'm now duped, I think I should be excused.

"As for your sash," Gavin declared, "may God repay you. I'll gladly wear it, not for its wonderful gold, not for its intricate woven wool, nor its side pendants, not for its cost or out of vanity, nor for its fine craftsmanship, but as a sign of my faults, wherever I go in success, remembering in remorse the corruption and frailty of the crabbed flesh, how prone it is to attract filthy stains of all kinds, and so when I get puffed up with an officer's pride, a little look at this *ceinture fléchée* will calm my heart.

"But one favour I'd ask of you, if you won't be offended, since you're Chief of these lands, here where you've so hospitably allowed me to stay–may the Great Spirit reward you–how do you pronounce your name right, and then no more questions."

"That I will truly tell you," the other one said. "In these parts I'm called Nuk-Luk, by some, Sasquatch. In England and Wales, and in all the British Isles, they know me as Wodwo, in the wilds of the Himalayas, Yeti. But in all Middle Eastern lands, I am called Al Khidr. Through the power of my wife, Changing Woman, whom you met in the lodge, I was sent in this shape to Arthur LeMagne, to try your spirit and terrify the high and mighty with a ghastly apparition, the one that spoke like a ghost and held his head in his hand before the head table. So I entreat you, my friend, come back to us, make merry in my house; my men love you, and I'm partial to you too, on my honour, as much as to any man on earth, because of your great love of truth. I'd invite you to be one of us, one of our tribe, and though I know your answer already, I'll extend the invitation anyway. Come visit the darkened lands where the solstice sun never rises. There you could drink from the fountain of youth and resolve whatever paradox besets you."

But Gavin told him no, in no way would he do that. And they embraced and kissed and commended each other to the prince of paradise, and before they parted right there in the cold, before that man in emerald green went wherever he chose, Nuk-Luk said, "If you see me dressed in green planing north down the River of Disappointment on a sturgeon's back, acknowledge me. If you see my aged wife wending her way west to meet her younger self and merge with her, send her your greetings. Think of us when children gather round the knees of their parents and when old men lie on their beds and contemplate the past.

And since you choose to remain human, recall just before dawn, when it is darkest, though the rivers threaten, they are merciful."

But Gavin McHenry, stubborn and humiliated, with a young man's stubbornness, humiliation, and rage for order, heard little of these blessings. His life spared by grace, over wild trails in the northern Nahanni, Gavin now trekked, Peowish in the lead. Sometimes he lodged in a trapper's cabin, but often outside in the cold, fought off animals in the valleys, bears and wolves, even moose, which at this time I don't plan to tell you about. The cut he'd got in his neck was healed, and not far from it, he wore the gleaming sash, like a brand round his body, the *ceinture fléchée*, his scarlet letter, but freshly green, not red!–bound at the middle, tied with a knot, in token that he'd been found stained by sin. In his pocket was the keychain he'd never parted with, his father's totem gift, with Solomon's star and Hecate's crescent moon.

And so, safe and sound, he arrived in Fort Simpson. Joy spread everywhere, and he was immediately flown to Arthur LeMagne's, where the last of that year's celebration before the tall Christmas pines still proceeded. Arthur embraced him, as did Ghylaine, and many of their smiling guests greeted him with pleasure, the Dene Grand Chief and Nelson Poundmaker too, asking how he had fared. He told of the strange things he'd had to endure, the trial at the chapel, Sasquatch's comportment, the lady's love, and at the end, the *ceinture fléchée*, that metisse thing that interwove life's precious strands with such dignity and grace. On his naked neck stood the wound he'd received at Nuk-Luk's hands, punishment for his dishonesty. Dismayed in the telling, he choked up for grief and rage. The blood rushed to his face in shame, as he showed them his scar.

"Look, sir," said the young man as he held up his sash, "This badge belongs with the mark on my neck, signs of the damage I've done and the sentence imposed for cowardice and covetousness that caught me up there, tokens of the lying I embroiled myself in. And I must wear it as long as I live, for man can conceal sin but never dissever from it, so when it's once fixed, it will never be worked loose."

Then Arthur consoled the young man with all of his guests, who, wiser in the ways of this world, laughed loudly about it and graciously agreed that in future, each lady and gentleman who came to the table, native or not, priest, officer, or businessman, should wear such a sash, a *ceinture fléchée* of bright green and gold, just like Gavin's, and worn round the waist for his sake. And that became part of the renown of Arthur LeMagne, and whoever wore it thereafter incurred an everlasting honour, as is recorded in the most reputable books of romance.

Hony soyt qui mal pence

ACKNOWLEDGEMENTS

Sasquatch and the Green Sash is a hybrid thing, at once an adaptation, translation, and Canadianization of the famous medieval work, *Sir Gawain and the Green Knight*. Many contemporary translations of this Middle English masterpiece are available, and I used a lot of them as guides, notably James Winny's facing page translation (Broadview Press, 1995), Keith Harrison (Oxford, 1998), and Brian Stone (Penguin, 1974), some of whose lines, like "For man can conceal sin but not dissever from it," in my view simply cannot be matched, so I stole them, shamelessly, I hope in the spirit of T. S. Eliot's sense of good and proper literary theft: "Mature poets steal; bad poets deface what they take."

I make particular acknowledgement of June Helm's splendid *The People of Denendeh: Ethnohistory of the Indians of Canada's Northwest Territories* (McGill Queen's University Press, 2000). Special thanks to illustrator Steve Adams, as well as to Professor K. S. Whetter of Acadia University and to novelist Robert Edison Sandiford for all help and guidance. Mistakes and infelicities remain entirely my own.